70, 71

Good-bye, My Lady ∽ ∽ ∽ ∽

Good - bye,

J. B. LIPPINCOTT COMPANY

Philadelphia   *New York*

JAMES STREET

My Lady

For
Mary Elliott

Good-bye, My Lady ∽ ∽ ∽ ∽

CHAPTER ∽ ∽ ∽ ∽ ONE

T HE SWAMP WAS SLEEPING THE NIGHT AWAY, BUT the boy was wide awake as he sat on the steps of the cabin and listened to the moonlight rhythm of things— the swish of the river around the cypress knees, the hum of insects, the low rumblings of the bullfrogs and the high cries of the wildcats.

A bull alligator bellowed up beyond the bend of the river and another answered from the sand-bar down the river and the boy judged their hiding places, for they were things to be hunted and sold.

Then he heard what he was waiting for: a haunting laugh that echoed across the bog and startled all the night creatures into silence, and then the swamp lay as still as unborn time and brooded resentment that its

symphony had been interrupted by a sound that did
not belong there at all.

Slowly, the boy got to his feet and cocked his head
toward the river and into the wind, and stepped noise-
lessly into the shadow of the cabin and waited with the
patience that comes with living in a wilderness of water
and trees.

For a long minute he waited, peering into the moon
shadows and then it came again: a chuckling yodel that
drifted off into a sob and ended in a weird "gro-oo-o."

The boy hugged the shadows as he sidled to the door
of the cabin and opened it and called softly, "Uncle
Jesse."

The old man sat upright in his bed and squinted toward the door. "That you, Skeeter? How come you
ain't asleep?"

"Heard it again, Uncle Jesse."

" 'Magination." The old man closed his eyes and
snorted. "Ain't nothing like a boy's 'magination, and
him growing."

"But I heard it again. This side the river. Heard it
plain as day."

The old man swung his feet over the side of the bed
and reached for his lantern and lit it. He put on his
shoes and pants and stuffed his long nightgown into his
pants, and he slipped on his denim jacket that he called

a swinky, a word brought across the sea by Uncle Jesse's forbears who came from Scotland's highlands and settled in this swamp more than two hundred years ago.

"Better put your shoes on." He held the lantern above his head and spoke to Skeeter. "Going in the swamp, you better put your shoes on."

"I'm all right. Let's get going while the moon's out." The boy felt in the corner by the door for an axe, a double-edged axe, and balanced it in his left hand and ran his right thumb across the edges. Wished he had a shotgun. A .20 gauge. Always wanted a .20 gauge shotgun.

Uncle Jesse put the lantern on a table and reached over his bed and took down his gun, a single-barreled .12 gauge, and broke it and put in a shell, and then he lifted the lantern and walked out of the door and into the night.

Skeeter followed him and they paused by the steps and stared into the swamp and Skeeter said, "Over that way." He nodded toward the river. "Heard it over yonder. Plain as day. Like a ghost laughing. Only it wasn't scary."

The old man grunted and set off down the path in long strides, his eyes to the ground in search of snakes, particularly the deadly cotton-mouth moccasins that

13

came out of the swamp and hunted along the path. The
boy was about three paces behind him and, in the re-
flection of the lantern, he, too, was watching for snakes,
always watching for snakes. The briars were of no
concern. The thick calluses of his bare feet took care
of that, but snakes were to be avoided.

He held the axe close to the head and in his left hand.
Yes sir-ree, bob-tail. Wished he had a shotgun. A little
old .20 gauge. A boy his age, sprouting up, needed a
shotgun. Cost $25, though. Get one next year, maybe.
Get one sure as shooting if they sold enough cord wood
or cypress knees or alligator hides or any of the things
that he and old Jesse Jackson got from the swamp and
sold in town.

They reached the east bank of the Pascagoula, the
muddy river that drains the swamp and flows into the
Gulf of Mexico at a nearby town that also is named
Pascagoula, and both town and river are in the southern
part of Mississippi. The river was at low stage and
deep within its banks, for summer was upon the land.

Uncle Jesse and Skeeter moved so silently that the
swamp creatures were not disturbed and soon their
sounds were at crescendo again, a thousand sounds stirring the swamp. The breeze was from the west, from
across the river, and then it shifted and was from the

south, from the Gulf of Mexico, and it was a fat wind, a damp one.

The boy felt the wind on the back of his neck where his tangled yellow hair hung low. He whistled softly and Uncle Jesse stopped and looked back at him and held the lantern high. Skeeter pointed up at the leaves moving and the old man watched them a second and grunted again.

Skeeter propped his axe against a log. "Wind's cut around to the south."

"Heard it up ahead, like you said?" Uncle Jesse turned the lantern low and put it on the ground and to the side of the path.

"Heard it right up yonder. Dead ahead and plain as day."

"Downwind from us now. Smell us sure." Uncle Jesse sat beside the lantern and relaxed. "Mout as well rest a little bit. Can't hunt nothing and it downwind."

The boy, also wise in the ways of swamps and animals, said not a word but sat by his uncle and watched the moon, and the clouds scuttling by it, and listened to the sounds. The fireflies were out with a million lights and the mosquitoes were out with a million daggers and the boy unbuttoned his shirt and pulled it over his head to protect his face from their torment. "Rain's heading in," he said. "Air's coming wet."

"Rain'll come on the east wind this time of year." Uncle Jesse raised his gaunt knees and rested his head on them and closed his eyes. "Wind'll be shifting to the east pretty quick now. Then we'll move on."

They waited. There was nothing to do but wait. Fox-fire glowed across the river and the river was slapping the cypress knees and suddenly the haunting laugh came again, and was close.

The boy's eyes were wide and staring. "That's it. Plum' nigh."

Uncle Jesse's mouth sagged open and he felt for his shotgun. "Great day in the mawnin'." Then he said it again. "Great day in the mawnin'. What is it?"

"No telling." The boy moved closer to the old man and gripped his axe. "Been hearing it every night for a week, like I said. And ain't no telling what it is."

The laugh drifted into an echo and the wind veered to the east. Uncle Jesse snatched up his lantern and the shotgun. "Come on."

The clouds separated wide from the moon and the moon was bright and the swamp was dappled in shadows except in a clearing by the river and there the light was mellow and without shadows. Uncle Jesse stopped, stock-still, and doused his lantern and held up his hand and glanced over his shoulder at the boy. He said not a word, but pointed toward the clearing.

Then Skeeter saw it and his heart pounded hard. Swamp born and reared, he feared nothing he could shoot or outwit, but here was something that scared him because he didn't know what it was.

The animal clearly was visible in the moonlight and was sitting on its haunches, and its head was cocked sideways and it laughed. It was a merry little chuckle, a rather melodious sound that came high like a yodel and then trailed off into a gurgling sob.

The Adam's-apple in Uncle Jesse's long red neck bobbed up and down like a fishing cork.

Skeeter's fear left him and he was pleased with himself because for days he had told his uncle that something strange was in the swamp and his uncle hadn't believed him, and here was proof that he had been right all along.

"Wonder what it is?" Uncle Jesse peered at the creature, studying it. He had no intention of shooting unless attacked and his curiosity had overcome his awe.

"Dog," the boy whispered. "Looks something like a little bloodhound whose mamma was a fox terrier or something."

"Looka yonder. Licking itself. Like a cat."

"Dog, I tell you."

"Mout'n. But don't no dog lick itself."

"That dog does. And go easy, it'll see us."

The old man and the boy slunk to the ground and crawled forward to a log and raised their heads above the log and watched the creature as it licked itself and then lifted its nose to the moon and chuckled. It was about a foot and a half high. Its coat was red and silky and there was a blaze of white down the chest and a circle of white around the throat. The face was wrinkled and sad, like a wise old man's.

"Dog," the boy insisted, careful lest his words carry to the clearing.

"Can't no dog laugh." Uncle Jesse was shaking his head.

"That dog can," Skeeter said. "I aim to catch it."

"Don't make sense." Uncle Jesse squeezed himself behind the log and looked at his nephew. "Laughing like a young'un and licking itself like a cat. Ain't natural."

The animal lowered its nose and turned and faced them, cocking its head from one side to the other.

"Smells us," Skeeter whispered.

"Can't nothing smell that far. Ain't even downwind, and if it was, can't nothing smell that far."

The animal crouched and braced and lifted its nose, and whipped it into the wind and froze to a point. Then it darted away, racing like a greyhound out of the clearing and into the swamp.

The old man and the boy swapped glances and Uncle

Jesse said, "Be John Brown. It did smell us. Can't nothing smell that far, but that thing did."

"Run like greased lightning, too." Skeeter stood up and looked toward the thicket into which the creature had disappeared. "Whatcha think, Uncle Jesse?"

The old man stood, too, and was tall and lanky, and he scratched his neck, rasping his calloused fingers against the sunburned skin. "Did that thing know what I am even about to think, it would have a running fit. A pure D conniption."

"Just the same, whatcha think?"

"That it ain't natural. Like a cross between a dog and a cat, and dogs and cats ain't supposed to cross." He glanced up at the moon and judged the time of night. "Mout as well go home. That thing is long gone, heading for the tall timber."

"Going to let it outsmart us?" Skeeter was disappointed because he was ready to hunt all night. "Like I told you, sort of figured on catching it."

"How you aim to catch something that can smell a mile and run like a scared rabbit?" Uncle Jesse picked up his lantern and turned up the wick and lit it. "That thing's a freak. Maybe got loose from a circus or something. I aim to ask ol' Cash about it. Ol' Cash knows everything."

He began moving away, back down the path, and the

boy continued to stare toward the swamp where the creature had vanished and then he ran down the path and caught up with his uncle. "Sort of hate to let Mister Cash in on it. You know how Mister Cash is."

"Ol' Cash is sharp as a briar." Uncle Jesse spoke without turning his head toward his nephew. "Knows something about everything, ol' Cash does."

"My hind leg!" the boy exclaimed. "All he knows is buy low and sell high. Loves a nickel mor'n a goat loves a gourd vine. You know that as good as me."

The man stopped and put his hand on Skeeter's head and tousled the long yellow hair. "Now, Skeeter, don't you go running down ol' Cash like everybody else. Best store-keeper in these parts. Friend, too. Sold us that saw on time, didn't he?"

"Yes, sir." The boy looked down at the ground and kept his thoughts to himself. He didn't like Mr. Alpheus Evans, who owned the cross-roads store in the nearby village of Lystra and who was called Cash because that's what he usually demanded, although he had sold Jesse Jackson a small circular saw on credit.

"So don't you go low-rating ol' Cash. Let us have that saw for $23.75, and been carrying us plum' nigh a year." He turned away from the boy and started down the path again. "Some day I aim to pay him. Some day I'm going to walk right in his store and put ever' frazzling bit of that money right on the counter and pay up." He was talking to himself as though he were alone, as though he believed what he said.

Skeeter was at his side and taking quick steps to keep up with his uncle's long, swinging strides and he scarcely heard the old man and yet he knew what he was saying because he had heard him say it so often. Really, he usually knew what Uncle Jesse was going to say before he said it because they lived so close together that each almost could read the other's thoughts.

For twelve years, since the boy was two, they had lived together in the little one room cabin by the river, and now the boy had grown into a willowy swamp sprout with tangled yellow hair that Uncle Jesse cut maybe once or twice a year. He had freckles too, and his real name was Claude.

His mother was Jesse's only sister and had died when the boy was a baby. No one thereabouts ever knew, or cared, what had happened to his father, an Alabama trapper who had drifted into the swamp and had drifted out again when his wife died. He did not want the responsibility of raising a motherless boy. And so Jesse Jackson, a leathery, toothless old man with faded blue eyes, had taken the baby to bring up and called him Skeeter because he was so little.

In the village of Lystra, where Uncle Jesse seldom

visited, folks wondered if he were fitting to rear a boy.
They thought him shiftless and no-count. Jesse Jackson
had lived all of his sixty years in the swamp and his ways
were a torment to people who believed that life must be
lived by their rules.

He earned a little money selling the things that he got
from the swamp—frogs and fish and saw-logs, stove
wood and muskrats; anything that he could get without
too much effort and sell without too much to-do. He
worked when he felt like it, but mostly he spent his days
paddling around the swamp and teaching Skeeter the
things that he thought were important: how to grab a
snake by its tail and snap off its head, why only female
holly trees have berries, why the Pascagoula river made
a humming, singing sound on certain moonlight nights—
things that he knew so well although he didn't know
much else, for Jesse Jackson could not read or write and
that failing was a misery to him and tormented him now
that he had his nephew under his roof.

The villagers might have tried to take Skeeter away
from the illiterate old swamper and send him to an or-
phanage, but for Cash Evans, the store-keeper. Cash was
a hard man, but fair. He often hunted with Jesse and,
when there had been talk of sending Skeeter away, Cash
had said, "Nothing shaking. That boy is a swamp sprout
and ol' Jesse is a swamp hickory and they belong to-

gether. Like seed and burr. Like sap and bark. Leave em be."

So that's all there was to it. Cash, however, did insist that Uncle Jesse send the boy to school in town when the roads were passable, but that wasn't regular and Skeeter attended classes only two or three days a week for five or six months a year, only in winter, of course.

He had reached the age of fourteen and knew almost nothing about life beyond the swamp and had heard only vaguely of such great places as New Orleans and Memphis and even Mobile, which was not very far away. New York and Chicago were fairy-tale names that he read sometimes in the old magazines and newspapers that Cash Evans fetched out to the cabin when he came to the swamp to hunt.

About a week before, Skeeter first had heard the strange night cry, the chuckling yodel that he knew did not belong in the swamp, and had told Uncle Jesse and the old man had scoffed at his story. But now they had seen it, a creature that looked like a dog but that laughed instead of barking, that licked itself like a cat and ran like the wind. Well, maybe next time Uncle Jesse wouldn't laugh at his story. That's what he was thinking as he walked beside the old man under the trees that dripped moss and held out their pale arms in the moonlight.

It was coming moondown when they got home, the moon wasting behind the trees and a few of the night things still about and calling sleepily: a lone jumbo frog that was too obstinate to accept the night's passing and too filled with himself to shut up, a night hawk on the ridge beyond the river, and a sandpiper running to the wing to meet the dawn at a hidden beach along the Gulf of Mexico where there was food for his craw and covering for his safety.

Skeeter stopped on the porch and drank from the water bucket there and Uncle Jesse went on inside and rested his shotgun on the two pegs above his bed and he lit the lamp and blew out his lantern, and sat on the bed and took off his shoes and rubbed his feet.

The boy came in, shedding his faded cotton shirt as he came through the door, and he propped the axe in a corner and sat on his bed and looked across at his uncle. "Mister Cash will try to hunt it down and maybe kill it. Want to catch it myself."

"Ol' Cash won't kill it less'n it's ornery."

"It ain't ornery. Been around a week. Been ornery, it would have pestered us. Just been minding its own business. You always say a thing's got a right to mind its own business."

Uncle Jesse slipped off his denim jacket and yawned and stretched. "Me and ol' Cash won't kill it less'n it jumps us. Get a few of his dogs come sun-up and run it and see what it is."

"Me too?" The boy continued to look across the room at the old man. "I'll be along?"

"You'll be along. Did I laugh at your story I'm rightly sorry. Said you heard it. Had no call to laugh at you."

Skeeter got up and moved the lamp from the stand by Uncle Jesse's bed and put it on the table near the little wood stove where they did their cooking. "Want I should fix a little breakfast?"

"Too early. Day-bust still a ways off. Mout as well get us some more sleep."

"Want I should get you a glass of buttermilk? Makes you sleep good. Buttermilk and raw onions make you sleep good. Heard you say so yourself many a'time."

"Getting to where onions give me the heartburn. Tell you what you can do, though. Do you don't mind."

"What's that?"

"Light up a few splinters to take the chill off the room. Sort of damp in here, and it hot summer."

Skeeter went to the wood box behind the cook stove and selected a few prime fat splinters and crossed over to the hearth and lit the splinters. They blazed quickly and he watched the hot tar ooze from the wood and then he laid the splinters in the fireplace and added a few sticks of stove wood and then a rich pine lightwood

25

knot. He sat in front of the fire watching the blaze turn from yellow to blue and then to yellow again and the shadows danced in the cabin and on Uncle Jesse and on the meagre possessions of an old man and a growing boy: two beds with cotton blankets and no sheets, the eating table of pine and the two chairs of hickory, the gun, the axe, and the lantern. And there the cook stove and against the wall nearby were propped a sack of flour and a sack of corn meal, and over the cook stove a shelf on which was kept sugar and salt and coffee, a can of baking powder, a bucket of lard and a can of milk. With land all around them and grass belly deep, they used canned milk instead of keeping a cow, for they were hunting folks and not farmers. Three times a week Skeeter rowed their skiff across the river and walked out of the swamp and across the west ridge and bought buttermilk from the Watsons, who were Negroes and whose elder son, named Gates Watson, had been away to school. The Watsons were good farmers and had cows and sold Uncle Jesse all the buttermilk he wanted, and the old man drank a heap of buttermilk and used the rest for cooking biscuits.

Uncle Jesse propped his elbows on his knees and cupped his chin in his hands and watched the boy sitting there by the fire and was sad that Skeeter was sprouting up. Soon his voice would go deeper into his throat and his lean arms would bunch into muscles at his shoulders and the cabin would be too small for him, and maybe the swamp, and then he would run to the wing and fly away as the sandpiper had done. Some day this would happen, some day soon, and the thought of it made the old man sad.

Skeeter sensed that Uncle Jesse was watching him. "Getting sleepy?"

"Not much. Rightly nice sitting here by the fire. Me and you."

The boy reached into a box on the hearth and spilled out some hickory nuts and began cracking them, carefully placing each nut on a brickbat used only for that purpose, and then cracking each nut with a smooth rock that Uncle Jesse had found many years before. They called it the nut rock. It almost was an automatic thing— the cracking—and Skeeter did it without thinking what he was doing, only waiting to get sleepy and for the fire to die down and for dawn to come.

"Like a few hicker' nuts?" He had collected almost a handful of the kernels.

"Reckon not," the old man said. He could not chew hickory nuts, for being without teeth he could not chew many things.

Skeeter selected the best of the kernels and mashed them to a pulp and handed the treat to the old man and

Uncle Jesse took it without a word, and relished it. If there was one thing in the world that he liked more than hickory nuts it was more hickory nuts. Some day, somehow, he was going to buy him a set of store-bought teeth —Roebuckers he called them—and then eat his bait of hickory nuts. But Roebuckers, even the cheapest kind, cost $65, and it might as well have been a million, so far was such a sum removed from old Jesse Jackson.

He got up from the bed and, barefooted, walked across the room and to the porch and got a dipper of water from the bucket there, and came back in and his long nightgown was flapping around his legs. He sat on the bed again and rocked back and forth. "Some day—"

Skeeter knew what was coming. He had heard it a hundred times.

"Some day I'm going to get me them Roebuckers. Sure as the good Lord made little apples, some day I'm going to walk right into ol' Cash's store and lay that money right on the counter and tell Cash to order them. Then I'm going to eat me a bait of hicker' nuts. And some roasting ears. Enough roasting ears to kill a goat. Maybe I can get me some Roebuckers with a couple of gold teeth in 'em. Seen a man once with six gold teeth."

Skeeter put the brickbat and the nut rock away and brushed the hickory nut shells into the fire and stood up. "I'm getting sleepy."

"Then go to sleep."

"Aim to." He took off his jeans and threw them across his bed where his shirt lay and crawled under the blanket.

Uncle Jesse blew out the lamp and glanced at the embers of the fire and then he, too, stretched out on his bed. "Good night, boy."

"Good night, Uncle Jesse."

"Say your prayers?"

"Saying them when you said good night."

"Ought to get on your knees to say your prayers. Do you get on your knees the good Lord pays more mind to what you say."

"You don't get on your knees."

"That's so. Say mine laying here in bed. Suits me and the Lord."

For a minute the room was in stillness and then the boy asked, "Whatcha pray for, Uncle Jesse? Them Roe-buckers?"

"Mostly." The old man didn't want to tell him the truth: that "I pray for you." It was not the thing to tell a boy.

Skeeter put his hands under his head and stared up at the rafters that were dimly visible in the glow of the embers. "Do you pray hard enough you'll get them. Read in a magazine about a praying man. Prayed up a storm."

29

"What'd he want?" Uncle Jesse asked.

"Rain. Got it, too. Flooded to beat all." The boy was very serious. "Just rained and rained and the river flooded and houses got washed away and cattle and stuff drowned. Reckon he prayed too much, Uncle Jesse?"

"Looks like it."

"Reckon I pray for a shotgun I might get it?"

"Mout'n."

"Then reckon I pray that I catch that thing out in the swamp I might catch it?"

"Mout'n."

"Do I pray for both what about that?"

"Too much praying. That's how-come folks get their-selves in a mess. Need a little ol' bitty shower, but they haul off and pray for rain and a flood hits 'em. Talking to the Lord is a thing to do easy. So don't never crowd Him, boy."

Again the room was quiet and they closed their eyes and sleep was almost upon them and both were thinking their own thoughts and of the things they wanted: the old man that the boy would grow up and be a fitting man and that he himself might have a set of store-bought teeth; and the boy that he could catch the strange crea-ture he had seen, a dog that chuckled instead of barking. And maybe a .20 gauge shotgun. He didn't know which he wanted most. He just didn't know.

CHAPTER ∽ ∽ ∽ ∽ TWO

I T WAS RAINING WHEN SKEETER WOKE UP AND HE LAY quiet a minute and listened to the wind in the water oak by the back door and the rain on the cypress roof. It was not full dawn, only half dawn, and the swamp was still and melancholy while the rain beat it; the rain that fed its springs and its roots and its river.

Even the mockingbirds were hushed, their feathers ruffled against the wet, and the jays were subdued and there was no greeting for the dawn. Nothing moved in the swamp except the river and the wind and the rain, and the rain dripped against the window by the boy's bed and he watched it and was pleased, for there would be no work today and it a'raining; and he might find time to slip away and catch the thing before Uncle Jesse could fetch Mister Cash and Mister Cash's dogs to hunt it down.

He heard Uncle Jesse on the front porch sloshing water on his face from the wash basin and he closed his eyes and played like asleep, hoping the old man would not call him until breakfast was ready.

Uncle Jesse came back into the cabin and stood by the bed and tugged the cover. "Aim to sleep all day?"

Skeeter flopped from his back to his side and his face was toward the window and he mumbled, "Raining."

"Is that a fact?" Uncle Jesse walked to the stove and shook down the ashes and laid splinters for a fire. "Called you once. Ain't calling you again."

The boy crawled out of bed with magnificent reluctance. "Can't work and it a'raining; outdoors nohow."

Uncle Jesse lit the fire and put on water for coffee and oatmeal and Skeeter slipped on his pants. Then he sat on his bed and yawned and looked at the world through eyes half closed; and the world was not good but only wet and dreary. He would give anything he owned to crawl back into bed, but then he didn't own anything except the breath that gave him life and the hope for the things he wanted.

And so he reached for his shirt and Uncle Jesse spoke again. "Do you can't work outdoors you work inside. Cleaning up maybe."

"Ain't dirty." Skeeter's voice was without animation and he felt put upon and abused: this chore of getting up at the break of day when the wind was singing everything else to sleep and the rain was dripping a lullaby.

Uncle Jesse measured the oatmeal and spilled it into a boiler of hot water. "Reckon I'll beat up some batter cakes." He was leaning over the stove and could have been talking to himself. "Nothing like batter cakes and it a'raining. Oatmeal and batter cakes and molasses."

Skeeter fluffed his pillow that was stuffed with goose feathers and straightened his blanket and his bed was made. "I ain't hungry much. Four, five batter cakes will hold me."

Uncle Jesse smiled inside of himself. "Rain'll be gone come good morn gloam. Then I'll go get ol' Cash and we'll beat the swamp for that thing."

Skeeter's eyes brightened and sleep was gone and he tucked his shirt into his jeans. "You forgot the salt again. Need a pinch of salt in that oatmeal."

"Wide awake." Uncle Jesse reached for the salt. "When a man's eyes and belly get together he's gen'ly wide awake. Now go wash your face. And hit those ears a couple of licks. Neck, too."

The boy flung open the door and stepped to the porch and the rain misted into his face. There was a hint of grey to the east, timid and uncertain, as the sun struggled up and Skeeter stepped to the edge of the porch and studied the clouds and knew that the old man was right, that the rain soon would pass. Be a bad hunting day, though. Ground wet and a trail hard to follow. Even Mister Cash's dogs would have trouble on a day like this and Mister Cash had the best dogs in the world, coming and going: fox hounds and hog hounds and coon hounds, bird dogs and squirrel dogs. He had a turkey dog too, the only turkey dog in the county.

Skeeter lifted the dipper from the bucket and poured a little water, a precious little, into the basin. The soap was nearby but he ignored it and was ready to dab the water around his eyes and mouth when Uncle Jesse yelled at him: "Close that door. Must have been born in North Carolina, never closing a door."

Skeeter closed it and returned to the basin and again Uncle Jesse yelled at him, louder this time that his voice could carry through the closed door. "That soap ain't fish bait. Use it. Water ain't scarce, neither."

The boy wondered how the old man knew and yet he always seemed to know. Uncle Jesse had eyes in the back of his head. So Skeeter filled the basin and picked up the soap and washed his face, even his neck and ears. It was better to do it now than to be sent back, and having done it he felt a tingle of achievement, that he had washed his face good the first go'round, that he had spared Uncle Jesse the trouble of sending him back.

He closed the door when he went back in and walked triumphantly up to Uncle Jesse and tilted his chin for an inspection of his neck, and the old man grunted approval. They sat down at the table and Uncle Jesse shoved a bowl of oatmeal before the boy and then a stack of batter cakes and watched him wade in. "Don't eat so fast," he admonished. "Ain't mannerable. And don't smack so loud."

"Forget. Get so hungry I just forget."

The old man himself had only coffee and oatmeal and he spooned the oatmeal into his mouth and then stared at the bowl. "Some day I'll get 'em and then do anybody ever say oatmeal to me again I'll bust him one. Going to eat me some real ham for breakfast, do I get my Roebuckers. Mess of ham big as both my hands. Some day, sure as the good Lord made little apples."

"Could I have a cup of coffee, Uncle Jesse?" Every morning the boy asked it.

"Nothing shaking. Too young. Coffee ain't good for young'uns. Makes their skin yellow."

"How big I got to be do I get a cup of coffee?"

Old Jesse Jackson turned the question in his mind and answered slowly. "Rightly big. Not big like in arms and legs and things like that, but sort of growed up inside."

"But when is growed up?" Skeeter had asked the question many times and seldom got the same answer and now he asked it mostly to please the old man, knowing that Uncle Jesse sort of expected him to ask it. He spread molasses on his last batter cake and crammed it into his mouth.

The old man had turned his face from the boy and was looking out of the window, his watery eyes unblinking as he watched the rain drip from the trees. And at last he spoke: "Maybe I don't rightly know how to tell you or maybe I just can't explain it. It's like a sapling growing into a hicker' nut tree."

Skeeter really was paying him no mind, for now that his stomach was full and a new day had entered his life his thoughts slipped from beyond the bare walls of their little cabin and soared high into the swamp and to the strange creature he had seen; the thing he wanted so much—now even more than a .20 gauge shotgun.

"Yes, sir—" Uncle Jesse's words trailed off and he stared down at his hands and at the dirt ground into his skin. The clouds were breaking up and the sun came squirming through, then wading through. "Where the woodbine twineth and the whangdoodle makes music all the day." His eyes brightened as though he had found something which had been lost a long time. "That's it. When you know why the woodbine twines and why the whangdoodle makes music, that's growed up."

This, too, Skeeter had heard before and was not impressed and he pushed back his chair. "Ain't no such thing as a whangdoodle. Just a saying."

"Maybe so." Uncle Jesse reached to the little table by his bed and got his pipe and lit it and the bowl gurgled as he puffed hard. "But maybe that thing out in the swamp is a whangdoodle. It sort of makes music."

"Whangdoodle, my hind leg. You just making up som'n. Come on, let's stack the dishes."

He put the dishes in a pan on the stove and Uncle Jesse walked to the front porch to get the water bucket and he left open the door as Skeeter had done, and then he remembered and shut it quickly and hard. He knew what was coming and sure enough the voice came from the cabin. "Don't slam the door. Must be a Yankee, always slamming doors."

Jesse Jackson grinned and lifted the water bucket and took it inside and they heated water and washed the dishes and then the rain was gone and the sun was out bright, and the summer day was fullborn. Uncle Jesse put his pipe and tobacco in his pocket and took his old felt hat from a peg and stuck five matches under his hat band. These were to be used for his pipe. He would sweat on them in his pocket. "I'll be going. Be sure and fill up the water bucket before I get back. But no hurry. Be back afore the sun starts wasting and I'll fetch ol'

Cash and his dogs and we'll start trailing that thing."

"I'll be ready." Skeeter dried his hands by rubbing them across his shirt. "Better pick up some stuff at Mister Cash's store. Baking powder and salt and things like that. Want we should make a list?"

"I'll remember."

Skeeter, however, knew better. A list was necessary for Uncle Jesse and yet a list was a delicate thing because it meant writing, and writing was a thing that Jesse Jackson did not understand. So Skeeter got the pencil stub and the tablet and put them on the table. "You make it out or want me to do it?"

Uncle Jesse rasped his fingers across the stubble on his chin and looked up at the ceiling as though debating the problem. "You do it. You need the practice." He stepped over to the shelf and examined the supplies. "Baking powder. Put down baking powder first."

The boy grasped the pencil and stuck his tongue out of the corner of his mouth and began writing. "Baking. Never can remember how you spell it. B-a. Ba. K-i-n. Kin. Bakin." He glanced up at Uncle Jesse for approval.

"That's baking all right. Plain as day." Uncle Jesse shoved his hat to the back of his head and was proud of Skeeter, and of himself. "Needn't put down powder. That's a jaw-breaker."

The boy shook his head and wet the pencil point on

38

his tongue. "But baking by itself sounds like bacon. We might mess it up. The store might be full of folks."

"Don't you fret." Uncle Jesse was confident. "Ol' Cash'll know we mean baking powder. I just put that list down on his counter, and he'll know."

That suited Skeeter. He had no idea how to spell powder and, of course, he couldn't ask Uncle Jesse. Nevertheless, the list must be right. Someone might see it and might laugh at Uncle Jesse if it were wrong and know that the old man could not read or write. Only a few people knew that he was illiterate— Mister Cash and the Watson family across the ridge, and the boy.

And so Skeeter prepared the list, laboring with each letter and chewing his tongue as he wrote:

Bakin.

Salt.

Lard.

Flower.

Tobaccy.

Then he read it aloud and Uncle Jesse nodded and pushed his hat even further on the back of his head. "Put down some candy. Jelly beans or maybe some of them chocolate drops."

"Chocolate drops?" The boy turned the word "chocolate" in his mind. Now there really was a jawbreaker. "Don't think much of chocolate drops. Now take gum

39

drops. I mean I rightly like gum drops."

"Me, too," the old man said quickly. "Always did like 'em. Chocolate drops ain't much. Put down gum drops."

The boy did, and with a flourish, and held the list up and examined his handiwork and was pleased. Uncle Jesse was safe even if someone saw it besides Mister Cash, and he was safe if he gave it to Mister Cash and did not try to show off by reading it.

He handed it to his uncle and the old man folded the list and put it in his pocket and they walked together out of the back door and to a woodpile nearby. It was pine wood and had been cut into fireplace lengths and now Skeeter must saw it into stovewood lengths. "Need about a cord today," Uncle Jesse said. "Ol' Cash will ask for that much and we better have it ready. Don't aim to owe him no more than we already do. Don't aim to stretch things."

"I'll cut a cord." It seemed so easy then, the day young and a swamp breeze fanning his face. "You start the motor."

The motor was an old truck with no tires or top. Uncle Jesse had traded for it and had hauled it to the cabin and he and Skeeter had jacked up the rear end and braced it on a stump. Then they had attached a belt to the left rear wheel and the belt to the circular saw that

Uncle Jesse had bought from Cash Evans, on credit. So the truck turned the saw and they were able to cut all the wood that the storekeeper wanted. It was a dilapidated arrangement, but it worked.

Uncle Jesse picked up the rusty crank from the ground and examined it. Some day he was going to clean it. Some day he was going to clean it bright with an oily rag. He inserted the crank and spun the engine and it caught and began wheezing. Skeeter set the carburetor for high speed and the wheel turned and the saw spun and bucked. "All set?" Uncle Jesse yelled above the spluttering and coughing of the motor.

"All set!" Skeeter yelled even louder than the old man. "You go ahead on. Me and this wood going round and round."

Uncle Jesse tugged his hat tight on his forehead and waved so long and took off down the path to the swamp and quickly was out of sight among the trees. Skeeter began sawing wood and the saw bit into the light pine and it made a high whine, a merry sound, and the sawdust flying clean and the wood falling under the saw. Yes, sir, he'd saw a cord. When Uncle Jesse and Mister Cash got back he'd have a cord all sawed and maybe even stacked. A cord wasn't so much. Just stick with it. That was the ticket. All he needed was spizzerinctum. That's what got things done. Spizzerinctum—stick to it.

That's what the school teacher always said. A little old spizzerinctum.

The sun came hot on his neck and on his yellow hair and sweat began trickling down his face and the gnats buzzed around his ears. He slapped at them and kept sawing and then he began singing:

"Thought I heard somebody say,
Soda pop, soda pop—take it away."

He tried his best to keep his mind on his work, on the wood and the saw, but soon he was leaning against the truck and gazing toward the swamp and wondering about the strange creature. Be funny if that thing walked right out of the swamp and up to him. Maybe if he ran to the swamp he might catch a glimpse of it. Be funny if he'd see it and whistle for it and it'd come to him just like a dog. Uncle Jesse's eyes would stand out like fried eggs. Now that would be something.

He counted the pieces of wood he had sawed and there were only fourteen. Slowly he stooped and lifted another log and slowly he pushed it against the saw and loudly he sang:

"Soda pop, soda pop—take it away."

Wished he had some soda pop. Lemon. He liked lemon soda pop. Strawberry was all right and root beer was fair to middlin' on a hot day, but give him lemon pop every time. Nehi. Get more in a Nehi. And thinking about it, his throat got dry. Drink of water might help. But there was no water in the bucket and he remembered then that Uncle Jesse had told him to fill it up. Engine needed water too. He wasn't looking for an excuse to quit so soon. No sir-ree. But the engine needed water and Uncle Jesse had told him to fill up the bucket. Ruin the engine to run it without water. Burn it up. Without the engine, the saw was no good and Uncle Jesse hadn't paid for the saw. Course he hadn't cut much wood and he didn't aim to knock off so soon, but the engine needed water.

He stepped around to the carburetor and tuned it low and let the engine idle and went to the cabin and got the bucket and swung off down the path toward the spring. Be funny if that thing came running out of the swamp along about now. He puckered his lips and whistled just for the fun of it and then stuck two fingers in his mouth and a whistle shrilled; so shrill that a peckerwood eased off pounding on an old dead oak and cocked his head and watched the boy. Skeeter picked up a clod and chunked at him, then swung on down the path.

The spring was near the river and Skeeter stretched on the ground and buried his face in the cool water and slacked his thirst. A dragonfly was darting among the reeds nearby and he filled his mouth with water and squirted it between his teeth and he missed the dragon-fly, but scared it away and the boy laughed. The pecker-wood was pounding again and the field larks were call-ing from the ridge beyond the river. The bobwhites too —whistling in the broom sage; calling loud and it sum-mertime.

He stretched out on his belly and looked at himself in the spring. His hair was matted. Uncle Jesse would be cutting it soon. Some day he was going into a barber shop and get a haircut. Just walk right in and sit in the chair and tell the barber to cut his hair. Big as you please.

He turned over on his back and stared at the sky and lay very still. Maybe that thing would come out of the swamp if he just lay still. Maybe it came right here to drink. That gave him an idea and he jumped up and looked around for tracks. Those were coon tracks. And there were turkey tracks. Sure as shooting. And a deer. They all came to the spring to drink, so maybe that thing did too. This was the place to catch it. He wouldn't tell Uncle Jesse or Mister Cash.

The Pascagoula river was singing that strange hum-ming music that makes it famous, that brings people from all around to hear the water sing and to wonder why. Like a swarm of bees, it sounded. Some folks said the noise came from fish, a sort of croaker that cried when the tide swelled in from the Gulf of Mexico and up the river. Others said the current made the sound as it sucked past a hidden cave. Others even said that it was gas escaping from the earth and into the river. But Skeeter knew that it was sand shifting across the hard slate bottom. He had heard it so often that now he paid it no mind, and turned his attention from the tracks around the spring to the spring itself.

The dragonfly was back and a swarm of mellowbugs darted on the water and he got on his hands and knees and leaned as far over the spring as he could and blew at them and they scattered.

"Mellowbug, mellowbug—come this way,
Then go back and do what I say."

He watched the waterbugs dash around the surface of the spring and sure enough one left all the others and scooted across. That was good luck if it turned around and went back. But the mellowbug tried to hide near the bank and that was bad luck and frantically the boy waved his hands over the water and whispered, "Dubs and venture dubs." That broke any evil spell.

Then he pulled a handful of grass and stirred the water. No harm in helping luck out a little bit. The bug slipped from under a leaf, circled and made a beeline for the other side, leaving a tiny ripple. The boy was delighted. That meant real good luck and now he could make his wish and it would come true. So he closed his eyes. Shotgun or the swamp creature? He had to make up his mind. There had been only one bug, so he got only one wish. For only a second did he hesitate and then he said aloud for the mellowbug to hear, "I want that thing. That's what I want."

For some reason he really expected the animal to walk right out of the swamp and up to him and maybe lick his hand. And so he sat and waited and he saw many things: a snake chasing a frog, a fish leaping in the river, a big log floating by, yet he did not see them at all because they were only shadows in his mind and left no impression whatsoever.

He had no idea how long he sat there, waiting and listening. The sun soared high and pierced through the trees and sparkled on the spring and then he remembered the wood and slowly he got up and filled the water bucket, and slowly he walked back to the cabin, still listening and looking. But the swamp showed him nothing that he had not seen before and told him nothing that he did not know. "Mellowbug, my hind leg. Just a saying. That's all it is. Never works."

He was hungry when he got home and ate a can of salmon and a handful of soda crackers and strolled out to the woodpile to resume his work. The engine long since had choked off and gasoline was dripping from the carburetor and it was flooded. Skeeter drained the carburetor as he had seen Uncle Jesse do and cranked the motor and was not aware at all of time and perhaps not even of place, as his mind was back in the swamp conjuring up fantasies. He would capture that creature single-handed and be a hero and he would tame it. Maybe he would take it to the town of Pascagoula and charge people to see it and make a lot of money and buy himself that shotgun and Uncle Jesse those Roebuckers. Or maybe he would join a carnival and travel plum' to Memphis.

The pile of stovewood was pitifully small and he was startled out of his daydreams by the sound of Cash Evans' truck and he was feeding wood rapidly to the saw when Mister Cash and Uncle Jesse came around the side of the cabin. Skeeter pretended not to see them, that he was too busy to see them.

Mister Cash called out to him and Skeeter stepped back from the saw and tried to act surprised that they had returned so soon. He felt Uncle Jesse looking at him and he did not look at Uncle Jesse. Mister Cash came up close and cut off the motor and squinted at the little pile of stovewood and kicked a few sticks aside, then took off his hat and scratched his bald head which was ringed by a fringe of thin sandy hair. He was not as tall as

Uncle Jesse and his little pot-belly folded over his belt.
There was a mole near his temple and out of it grew
three red hairs. His voice had a rasping sound like the
grating of a file and his eyebrows joined at the bridge
of his nose and were bushy.

"Call that a cord of wood?" He kicked aside a few
more sticks and glowered at Skeeter. "Jesse said you'd
have a cord. And what you got ain't no-count. Not
even for selling purposes."

Only then did the boy look at Uncle Jesse and quickly
the old man stepped to his side and ran his finger across
the teeth of the saw. "Be John dog! Wouldn't cut hot
butter." He nudged a stick of wood with his foot.
"How'd you cut so much wood with such a dull saw?"
He did not give Skeeter a chance to answer, but turned
to the storekeeper as though he were the culprit. "That
saw ain't worth a hooray, Cash. Work myself to a frazzle
to keep it sharp and oiled, and it dulls up after a few
little old sticks of stovewood."

Cash Evans braced himself in front of Uncle Jesse and
his neck flushed red like the wattles of an angry turkey.
He pushed himself up close to the old man and his little
pot-belly shook his wrath and bounced up and down.
"You owe me a cord of wood, Jesse Jackson. Let you
have them groceries on time and I want my wood."

"Now don't bust a trace, Cash. You'll get your wood.

48

But you can't hold a boy to a cord and him with a dull saw." He stooped and picked up a stick of the wood and spoke his praise of how cleanly it was cut and then he spoke directly to Skeeter. "Saw broke down again, huh? All time breaking down, ain't it? Man ought to be shamed of himself for putting a no-count saw like that off on a fellow."

Cash Evans stepped back and looked at the old man and the boy, and spluttered indignation. He had sold Uncle Jesse the saw in good faith and now he was being abused because a daydreaming boy had dawdled. "That saw didn't break down, did it, Skeeter?" He knew that Uncle Jesse was capable of doing strange things to the truth, but the boy was different and so he put the question direct. "Nothing wrong with that saw, now is it? You just messed around."

"Engine was fixing to get hot." Instinctively he sided with Uncle Jesse, perhaps to protect himself. "Had to go get water." He walked over to the back steps and sat in the shade. "Bring your dogs, Mister Cash?" He changed the subject so skillfully that Uncle Jesse smiled and put his hand over his mouth to hide the smile.

"Course I did." Most of the anger left Cash Evans and he joined Skeeter on the steps. "Jesse tells me you jumped som'n out in the swamp. A regular scutter, or a whangdoodle or som'n."

The boy stretched out his legs and relaxed and Uncle Jesse propped against the cabin and, of course, in the shade. "Ain't no telling what it is." Skeeter was very conscious of being the center of attention. "But you'll get it. Never saw you miss nothing yet. Not with your dogs. Best dogs in the county, Mister Cash. You got the best dogs in the county."

Cash Evans was disarmed completely, for he could not be put out with anybody who bragged on his dogs. "They do pretty good, them dogs of mine. Let's get going."

Uncle Jesse joined in the talk. "Maybe me and Skeeter ought to stay here and finish that cord."

"That's so," Skeeter said. "We promised a cord."

"Blazes with that stovewood," Cash said. "Let's get to hunting. Come out here to work my dogs."

Skeeter caught Uncle Jesse's glance and was silent and the old man took his pipe from his pocket and slowly knocked out the ashes against the sole of his shoe, and filled the pipe and lit it. "Now, Cash, it was you who said it. So don't be thinking me and the boy weren't all set to finish the deal."

The storekeeper was bested and he knew it, and shook his head and grunted. "I'll get the wood later. Let's get going. Soon be pink of evening."

"Won't take *your* dogs long to catch that thing."

Then Skeeter turned to Uncle Jesse. "Say you got them groceries?"

"Sure he did." Cash did not wait for Uncle Jesse to reply.

"And how about the list?" Skeeter asked. "Wasn't that a humdinger?"

"Good as I ever saw." Cash glanced over toward Jesse and their eyes met and then each looked away from the other. "Been tending store all my life and never saw a better list."

"Now you talking." Uncle Jesse was beaming. "And tell him how I walked right in your store and thow'd that list right on the counter, and all them folks around."

"Is that a fact?" Skeeter asked eagerly.

"It's the Lord's truth," Cash said. "You oughta seen it. Store full of folks and your Uncle Jesse walked right in big as you please and thow'd that list on the counter so everybody could see it, and I picked it up and read it out loud and I said 'Good a list as I ever saw. You sure wrote up a good list, Jesse.' Ain't that what I said, Jesse?"

"That's what you said. Plain as day. They all heard it, too. Every frazzling one of 'em."

Skeeter was relieved that Uncle Jesse had not been embarrassed and wanted to thank Mister Cash and might have, but the storekeeper spoke first. "Beings you brought up the list—" He fixed his eyes sternly on the boy. "You messed up baking. It's b-a-k-e. Bake. I-n-g. Ing. Baking."

The boy felt the blood mounting to his cheeks and fumbled with his hands.

"Spell it," Cash said.

It was done.

"Now powder. P-o-w. Pow. D-e-r. Der. Powder."

That, too, was done, and Cash solemnly nodded approval and then Uncle Jesse nodded approval, even more solemnly. "And don't forget it," Cash ordered. "I won't be telling you again. Messed up flour, too, but we'll get that later."

"How 'bout tobaccy?" Skeeter asked. "That's a jawbreaker."

"Ain't that a fact?" Uncle Jesse had to join in.

"Had it right," the storekeeper said.

"Told him so," said Uncle Jesse. "Anybody knows how to spell tobaccy."

"Let's get going," Cash said impatiently. "Dark'll catch us."

The boy ran into the cabin and got his axe and the shotgun and broke the gun and put in a shell and joined the men in front of the cabin. "Maybe you rather tote the axe," he said hopefully to Uncle Jesse.

"I'll take the gun."

So Skeeter handed the gun to the old man and they

walked out toward Cash's truck and dogs began baying in the truck. Cash hurried ahead and climbed to the bed of his truck and untied the first hound, a mottled dog with sleepy eyes and a long cold nose. The dog bounded out of the truck and began circling the cabin, sniffing the ground and then lifting his head into the wind.

"What kind is he, Mister Cash?"

"One of them *any* dogs. Do anything. Runs coons, rabbits, even foxes. Fastest dog in the county. He'll catch that thing."

"Hurt it?"

"Mor'n likely not. Just tree it."

Skeeter watched the hound race into the woods behind the cabin and out again. "What's his name?"

"Gabe. When he starts baying it's like Gabriel blowing his horn. So I named him Gabe." Cash untied two other dogs and snapped leashes on them and pulled them out of the truck. They were big red dogs and were sullen and morose.

Skeeter gripped his axe and stepped back and Uncle Jesse slipped his gun off safety and moved close to the boy.

"Ain't as bad as they look." Cash held the leashes tight and the dogs raised their heads and sniffed and their eyes were bloodshot and their mouths hung open, showing their fangs.

Hog dogs. Big, tough brutes bred especially to hunt wild hogs in the swamp. Skeeter was scared. That thing wouldn't have a chance against those dogs. He looked pleadingly at Uncle Jesse and the old man said, "Cash won't turn them loose less he has to. Ain't that so, Cash?"

"Not unless I have to." He squatted by his hog dogs and stroked them. "Bark and Bellow. They're named Bark and Bellow. Kill a bear if they jump him."

Skeeter swallowed hard and there was a sickening feeling in the pit of his stomach. "That thing ain't big much. And he ain't hurt nothing. Just a dog that don't bark. Just sort of laughs instead of barking. Ain't so big."

"Size don't count." Cash straightened up and whistled and Gabe came from behind the house. "I aim to find out what it is. If Gabe can't get it, then I'll turn loose Bark and Bellow."

"But it ain't hurt nothing," Skeeter said. "Them hog dogs will kill it." Again he turned to Uncle Jesse. "You won't let them kill it, will you? It's sort of mine. I heard it first, Uncle Jesse. You don't aim to let Mister Cash turn them hog dogs loose on it? Little old thing that ain't hurt nothing."

"I'll be nigh," Uncle Jesse said. "But we got to get it. Mout be dangerous."

Cash called Gabe close to him, but held the hog dogs tight, and waved his arm toward the swamp and Gabe loped away in that direction. "Whole thing sounds crazy to me. Do the Watsons know about it? They're rightly smart for colored folks. 'Specially Gates."

"Don't know if they know or not," Skeeter said.

"That Gates'll know what it is if anybody knows. He's been plum' up to Alcorn A. & M. College. Ever see them books he reads?"

"Yes, sir."

"Thick as my arm. Writes mighty fine, too, Gates does. And can spell anything."

"That's a fact."

"Course some folks—" He squinted at the boy. "Some folks don't mind colored folks knowing mor'n them. 'Bout spelling and such. But me, I don't like it."

The boy didn't reply.

"Your Uncle Jesse says that thing looks like a dog—"

"It is a dog," Skeeter said.

"But laughs instead of barking? Licks itself like a cat?" Cash grunted his disbelief. "If you all telling me the truth, I aim to have it. If I got to run it from here to Mobile, I aim to have it."

He reached into his truck and lifted out his heavy rifle and balanced it in the crook of his right arm and held the hog dogs with his left hand. They saw the rifle and raised their heads high and growled and Cash led them toward the swamp and toward the clearing where

Skeeter and Uncle Jesse had seen the thing.

Uncle Jesse put his gun back on safety and glanced at Skeeter as though to reassure him and they walked off, Cash and his hog dogs leading the way, and then Uncle Jesse, and then the boy, gripping his axe and feeling his heart against his ribs.

From away in the swamp came a high call from Gabe, a ringing bay. "He's casting," Cash said. "When he hits the trail he'll bay low." The hog dogs trembled their floppy ears and strained at the leashes and their mouths drooled wet.

Skeeter shuddered, and then he remembered the mellowbug and made another wish: this time that the strange little thing would get away.

CHAPTER ∽ ∽ ∽ THREE

G ABE WAS RANGING FAR UP THE EAST BANK OF THE
river and out of sight and the three hunters walked in
single file along the path, Cash holding his hog dogs
tight and Uncle Jesse with his neck bent and his head
bobbing as he walked. He seemed to be watching the
ground but often he turned his head a bit and glanced
at Skeeter, and, in a way, he was sorry they had brought
the boy along.

Skeeter himself was dejected and down in the mouth.
He kept feeling that the thing didn't have a chance and
that made him miserable. He wished he was back at the
cabin and that he wouldn't have to see what he expected
to see; and, yet, if he turned around and went back
Mister Cash might think that he was scared and not big

57

enough to hunt with men.

The wind was from upriver and the hog dogs caught all the smells it bore and kept their noses close to the ground and trembled their eagerness. Cash spoke sternly to them. "Easy now. Hold it. Hold it, you Bark. Easy now, Bellow."

Like Uncle Jesse, he sensed Skeeter's mood and he, too, was sorry that the boy was along. He twisted his head over his shoulder and called back to Skeeter: "How the muskrats this year?" Anything to get Skeeter's mind off of his troubles and to lighten his spirits.

"Fur's mighty thick and it summer," Skeeter called back and was proud that his opinion had been asked.

"Means a hard winter," Uncle Jesse said.

And they walked on, their ears tuned for the first deep bay from Gabe which would be the signal that he had jumped something and that the race was on.

"How about alligators?" Cash asked. "Heard any 'gators?"

"Heard a couple," Skeeter said. "Big 'uns. Bulls."

Cash Evans did not ask where he had heard them. That would have been like asking a cattle man how many steers he had or a banker how much money he had. It just wasn't done. "I can always use 'gator hides," the storekeeper said. "Bee gums, too."

58

"Bears rob all the bee gums," Uncle Jesse volunteered. He had been out of the conversation long enough. "Swamp's full of bears."

The ground was spongy under their feet and then they were out of the swamp and into a clearing and Uncle Jesse looked at Skeeter and the boy said nothing, and so Uncle Jesse said, "This is where we seen it, Cash. Right over yonder, licking itself like a cat and laughing."

Cash tied Bark and Bellow to a tree and cupped his hands and shouted into the wind, "Heah, Gabe. Heah. Heah."

Skeeter sat on a log and rested his axe between his legs and Uncle Jesse sat beside him and propped his gun against the log, and slowly ran his fingers over the back of his left hand and stared at his hands.

Gabe broke out of the swamp and into the clearing, loping easily, and he came up to Cash and the storekeeper waved him away, and he began circling. He worked to the edge of the clearing and back again, his nose hard to the ground and his tail whipping.

"Got a merry tail," Uncle Jesse said. He had to brag on the dog. It was the polite thing to do and Cash expected it. Besides, Gabe was a good dog.

Skeeter watched the hound casting, covering the clearing fast, pausing to tilt his nose high and sniff the

59

breeze and then lowering his nose and working over the ground; methodically, surely. "Fast, all right." Skeeter said it with authority, for he was in the company of men and he spoke as a man should.

"Fastest in the county." Cash came over to the log and sat down and looked over at his hog dogs and calmed them and then gave all of his attention to Gabe, calling encouragement as the hound sought the trail; ranging across the clearing, pausing and wheeling, and his cold nose trembling in the breeze.

"Taking him quite a spell to get it," Skeeter suggested. There was a hint of longing in his tone, and hope.

"He'll get it." Cash said without brag, but in the awful finality of expert judgment, the undisputed wisdom of a man grown.

Uncle Jesse said nothing, for he, too, found himself hoping that Gabe would miss the trail.

The big hound obviously was baffled and Cash shook his head and frowned. "Never knowed him to take so long. Som'n wrong."

"He's messed up." Skeeter had been wanting to say it and now he said it. "That thing's just another dog and Gabe ain't used to hunting dogs. We might as well go home. That thing's long gone."

The words scarcely were spoken before Gabe braced

himself and his long ears arched. Cash jumped to his feet. "He's got it! Watch him work. He's got it!"

The hound throated one quick bay and was off, bounding across the clearing and toward the swamp up the river. Uncle Jesse stood, too, and watched the dog vanish into a canebrake and then into the swamp, and Skeeter stood on the log and watched and his heart was pounding.

Gabe's voice came ringing clear and was high and musical, his yelps of joy and excitement as he settled to his work of running down the smell that tantalized him. The swamp echoed his song and all the birds hushed. The hog dogs began growling and pulled hard on their chains.

"Got som'n," Uncle Jesse said. "Sure as the Lord made little apples."

"Maybe a fox." Skeeter still was hopeful. "Singing like he's jumped a fox."

"Ain't no fox." Cash grinned his pride. "Singing a new song. Jumped that thing." The storekeeper stepped over and untied the hog dogs' leashes from the tree. They looked up at him as though begging to be freed and their tongues hung long and their lips quivered over their fangs. "Whoa up," Cash commanded. "You'll get your lick at it. Whoa up."

He led Bark and Bellow back to the log and Skeeter

gripped his axe and stared at them and hated them. He liked Gabe—the singing was far up the swamp now—he liked Gabe singing his work song and earning what he found, but he hated the hog dogs that just waited for their victim. Gabe knew how to hunt and hold, but these things knew only how to hunt and kill.

"Running upriver," Uncle Jesse said and without spirit, for now that the race was on he had no heart for the chase. "Aim to follow him?"

"Not unless he trees," Cash said. "Mor'n likely Gabe will circle that thing back this way. We'll just wait."

The hound's song grew fainter and fainter and the hunters knew that Gabe was being led far upriver and into the deepest swamp. He was still trailing and racing, his song the rhythm of a dead run chase. Uncle Jesse put his hand behind his left ear and bent his ear into the wind. "Gabe ain't even about to tree. That thing is running hard. Whatever it is, it's running hard."

Skeeter said nothing, but his lips were tight and his hands were closed so tight that his fingernails bit into the palms of his hands, and he was wishing to himself and praying for the magic of the mellowbug to save the thing and let it get away.

Cash squatted between Bark and Bellow and stroked their heads to quiet them, all the while listening to the calls of his trailing dog, far away and very faint. "Mor'n likely it's heading for water. Can't run long like that."

"Gabe's got sense enough to head it off from water," Uncle Jesse said. "He won't let it get to the river."

"Mor'n likely its tongue hanging out now," Cash said. "Dragging the ground. Bet ol' Gabe done run its tongue out." He straightened up and looked back down-river where the cabin was, and the spring. "It'll head for the spring, mor'n likely. Bet that's where it's been drinking."

"Oh, no, it ain't." Skeeter spoke up quickly and his lips quivered, and he fought back his tears. "It don't drink there."

"How you know?" Cash demanded.

"Was at the spring this morning. Looked all around. It don't drink there."

Cash reached for his rifle and mumbled to Bark and Bellow and then said out loud, "I aim to see. We'll go to the spring."

Uncle Jesse glanced at Skeeter and then looked up at the sky and away from Cash and yet he spoke to the storekeeper. "The boy said it don't drink at the spring. And if the boy said it, that's how it is."

Cash was surprised at the hard tone of the words and squinted at his old crony. "What's eatin' you? Act like you don't want to catch it. Said I'm going to the spring, and I aim to go—"

63

"They're heading back!" Skeeter yelled it out and jumped up on the log and was nearer to the hog dogs than he had intended to be. "They're running this way and circling."

Gabe's bay came faintly clearer and then loudly clearer, first from upriver and then to the east, and it was deep and rumbling, almost a panting bay.

"Headin' for the spring!" Cash's voice was a high whine and he was so excited that his eyes popped. He dropped his rifle and began stroking his hog dogs, and they were clawing the ground to be away and to the hunt. "Gabe's right on it and it's running for water. Told you ol' Gabe would run it down. Told you so."

Uncle Jesse stepped up on the log beside Skeeter and peered into the direction of the chase, the song coming clearer and about a quarter of a mile away. "Sounds like Gabe's sort of tuckered. Singing bass. Like he's panting. Like he's perishing to death."

"Tuckered my hind leg!" The sweat popped out on Cash's forehead and he jumped up and down and could not restrain himself but cupped his hands and yelled to his hound. "Get him!" Gabe was too far away to hear, but Cash yelled again, screaming it. "Get him! Get him, Gabe!"

Skeeter was the first to see the thing when it broke out of the swamp and he raised his hand to point and

tried to shout, but no sound came and he stood on the
log, his mouth open and his eyes wide and his hand
shaking as he pointed across the clearing. A throb
surged from his stomach to his backbone and tingled
up his spine and the shout was choked in his throat.

The hunted stranger raced into the clearing, loping
easily with its chest low and its tail poker stiff. Gabe
was nowhere in sight. "Yonder it is!" Skeeter found his
voice and he, too, started jumping up and down and
yelling. "It outrun Gabe! Yonder it is!"

"Be John dog!" Uncle Jesse saw the thing and was
so excited that he slipped off the log and then jerked
off his hat and beat it against his leg. "Beat ol' Gabe!
Run him ragged! Cuted him—sure as shooting."

Cash Evans simply could not believe what he saw and
what he heard: the strange quarry running across the
clearing and toward them while Gabe was still in the
swamp baying frantically, but far behind. Cash's jaw
twitched and he spluttered and his face and neck flushed
red and sweat poured from his face. Bark and Bellow
pulled their leashes so tight that their necks swelled and
they were choking themselves, and drooling.

The thing kept coming straight and seemingly was
unafraid, running toward the men with the confidence
of a friend, as though they were protection from the
baying brute back in the swamp. Skeeter wanted to call

out to it or to whistle, but he wasn't sure that was the thing to do. He was too excited to think clearly and leaped from the log and started toward the clearing to meet it.

Uncle Jesse grabbed his arm. "Can't smell us. We're downwind—"

"It sees us!" Skeeter protested. "Bound to see us and it's coming to us."

Gabe ripped out of the swamp and into the clearing and the hog dogs were beside themselves with fury and it was Bellow that raised his nose and rumbled a deep bay. Instantly Cash unsnapped the leashes and the hog dogs lunged forward.

The little stranger stopped and raised its head and looked at the men, first in assurance and then in wonderment and then in bewilderment. For a second it stood there trembling and then, suddenly aware that it was alone and without friends, it wheeled to dash away, but Gabe was coming in fast, baying low and triumphantly.

Bark went straight for the victim while Bellow circled to the right and the little thing was trapped between the hog dogs and Gabe. Skeeter wanted to cover his eyes and yet he was fascinated. Uncle Jesse's mouth was a thin grim line and Cash was staring at the scene and breathing heavily.

66

Bellow attacked first. He grumbled his challenge and Gabe checked himself, honoring the warning and awaiting his turn. The little stranger braced and the hog dog bounded in for the kill.

Skeeter screamed. He could not help it, and Bellow, hearing the scream, jerked up his head, exposing his neck for one split second. The hunted creature leaped. A flash of red, then the cold white of its fangs and it was at Bellow's throat, ripping and tearing.

The big dog fell back, growling his pain. Then Bark lunged in, attacking low. The thing leaped aside and spun and raked the hog dog's flank as he flashed by. Gabe coiled and was ready to move in.

"No!" Uncle Jesse picked up a stick and started forward. "I won't take no more of it—"

He never finished the sentence, for Cash shouted a command to Gabe and then to Bark and Bellow. "Come heah! Dad blame it! Come heah!"

His dogs looked at him uncertainly, as though they could not believe his words or his tone, and they dropped their guards and the thing sounded that haunting laugh and leaped cleanly over Gabe and was away, fleeing for the swamp and safety.

"It's gone," Skeeter yelled. "Got away!"

"Come heah! You heard me. Come heah. You slab-sided devils." Cash repeated the commands and his dogs came to him, the hog dogs licking their wounds and Gabe crawling along the grass in abject humiliation.

Uncle Jesse threw away the stick and picked up his hat that had fallen beside the log. "You called off your dogs. Let that thing get away."

"Durn right I did." The storekeeper snapped the leashes on his hog dogs and waved for Gabe to head for the cabin. "That thing's a dog. The boy was right."

"And he outrun Gabe." Skeeter felt tears in the corners of his eyes and hoped the men didn't see them.

"Stood up to my hog dogs," Cash said. "Both of 'em." He took out his handkerchief and rubbed it across his sweaty face. "And now I tell you som'n. Anything that can outrun Gabe and that'll jump my hog dogs— well, I ain't messing with it. It's got a right to live. I say let it stay loose like the good Lord made it." He put his handkerchief back in his pocket and picked up his rifle. "Going home. Know when I'm whupped."

Skeeter loved Mister Cash then; almost as much as he loved Uncle Jesse. "I'll tote your rifle, Mister Cash."

"Tote it myself."

"Then I'll hold your dogs. I ain't a'scared of them hog dogs. Want I should hold them?"

"Hold 'em myself."

Uncle Jesse took the shell out of his shotgun and blew down the barrel and then took out his shirt tail

68

and rubbed the barrel. "That thing sure did outrun Gabe. Made him look like he was standing still."

"Ain't arguing." Cash wrapped the leashes around his hand. "Come on, Bark. You, too, Bellow."

They moved away out of the clearing and into the path that led to the cabin. Uncle Jesse handed his shotgun to Skeeter and took the axe himself. "That thing sure did whup them hog dogs."

"Told you I ain't arguing," Cash said. "But he didn't whup 'em. Just f'out 'em. And sort of nicked 'em."

"Sure would cause talk." Uncle Jesse rubbed the stubble on his chin. "Folks around your store be rightly perted up. Sure would cause talk. Little ol' thing like that outrunning Gabe and whupping your hog dogs."

Cash looked over at the old man and grunted, and walked on.

"Been thinking." Uncle Jesse put the axe over his shoulder and tilted his hat to the back of his head. "That saw you sold me ain't worth a hooray. Ain't worth more than two, three dollars."

The storekeeper stopped and spoke to his dogs and made them lie down and he took off his hat and ran his fingers across his bald head. "Tell you som'n, Jesse. You ain't saying nothing about this. I'm just telling you."

"Sure would cause talk," Uncle Jesse said slowly.

"So would that list Skeeter wrote. And all them other

lists that you bring to my store. And all the big talking you do about how you read to the boy instead of him reading to you." Cash's tone was so serious that Skeeter looked at him quickly and knew that he meant every word he said.

"Aw, now wait a minute." Uncle Jesse's mouth drooped and he retreated, and was ashamed that the boy should hear this. "You ain't going to tell on me. We been friends a long time. Me and you. You just funnin', huh, Cash? Don't like to hear you talk that way."

"Then don't low-rate my dogs. Don't let nobody low-rate my dogs. You ain't telling on my dogs and I ain't telling on you."

"Sure are good dogs." Skeeter stepped immediately into the role of peacemaker.

"Who's low-rating your dogs?" Uncle Jesse pretended surprise and there was a hurt look on his face that he should be accused of such a thing. "I wasn't aiming to big-talk."

"And I'm sick and tired of you running down that saw," Cash said. "We traded fair and square and you owe me $23.75."

"Fair and square," Uncle Jesse said meekly.

Skeeter knew that the storm had passed and his steps were lighter. He swung the gun across his shoulder and carried it proudly. The thing was safe and he was walking with men and he had been right all along: the thing was a dog and his mellowbug wish had come true.

They reached the cabin and night was coming, and Uncle Jesse asked Cash to share supper with them.

"That's rightly nice of you," the storekeeper said. "But I'll be getting on back."

Skeeter ran into the cabin and sliced off some bacon rind and brought it out and gave it to Cash. "They're mighty good dogs, like I said."

Cash sat on the steps of the cabin and stroked his dogs and gave them the bacon rind. "They do all right. They're my dogs." He got up and walked out to his truck and Skeeter and Uncle Jesse went with him, and he fastened his hog dogs in the bed of the truck and climbed behind the wheel and called to Gabe to sit beside him. "I ain't saying nothing about that thing back yonder in the swamp. Somebody mout hunt it down." He ran his hand across the windshield, wiping off some of the dust.

"I'm rightly obliged," Skeeter said. "Sort of feel like it's mine. Me seeing it first."

"It's yours. Far as I figure—it's yours." He reached out and tousled the boy's yellow hair. "Now, how you spell baking powder?"

Skeeter pondered a second. "B-a-k. Bak. I-n-g. Ing.

Baking. P-o-w. Pow. D-e-r. Der. Powder."

Uncle Jesse put his pipe in his mouth but did not light it. "That's baking powder all right. So long, Cash. Come back any time."

He and Skeeter stepped back and Cash drove away in a cloud of dust and then the old man and the boy walked slowly to the porch and Uncle Jesse said, "Wash your face and hands. I'll be fixing supper. And don't slam the door when you come in."

The boy covered the bottom of the wash basin with water and ran his finger back and forth through the water and was not thinking what he was doing, for his thoughts were back in the swamp. He looked up from the basin and toward the river, staring that way, and the night things were coming out again, crying and wailing and humming. Mosquitoes were rising and he slapped at them and then tapped water around his mouth and on his cheeks and reached for the floursack towel on a nail by the basin.

He was reluctant to leave the porch and the outside sounds but he heard Uncle Jesse rattling the plates and setting the table and he opened the door and went in and closed the door without slamming it. Uncle Jesse was heating a can of beans and four corn pones were browning on the top of the stove, simple bread of corn meal and salt and water. The old man was cooking in the soft light of late dusk, the evening gloam drifting through the windows.

Skeeter lit the lamp and put it on the table and Uncle Jesse tasted the beans and nodded without speaking, and emptied most of the beans into the boy's plate. He put a corn pone before each of them and a cup of coffee before himself and they began eating and were silent. Bugs were darting around the lamp and many of them died there against the hot chimney and in the little yellow flame.

Uncle Jesse kept watching Skeeter, raising his eyes from his food to look at him, but it was the boy who spoke first. "How come you cook four hunks of bread? Gen'ly we get by on two."

"Reckoned you mout be hungry."

Skeeter was eating his beans with a spoon and caught his uncle's eye and licked the spoon clean and put it down and began using his fork. "Be obliged if you'll let me cook up a slab of middlin' meat. A pretty good slab."

"You ain't *that* hungry?" The old man poured some of his coffee into his saucer and blew on it and drank it. "What's on your mind?"

"Maybe you won't need me tomorrow." He did not answer the question directly, but sort of sidled into his answer.

"That cord's got to be cut." Uncle Jesse used his knife to scrape out the soft inside of the pone because the crust was too hard for him. "But I reckon I can cut it by myself. What's eating you?"

"Maybe I'll go out and get that thing." Skeeter did not look up from his food and tried to make his words sound casual.

"By yourself?"

"Yes, sir."

Uncle Jesse took another swallow of coffee and scraped back his chair and went to the shelf and took down the meat. He cut off a hunk and held it up. "Reckon that'll do it?"

"Yes, sir." The boy finished his beans and pushed his plate aside. "I'll boil that and pour the potlikker on them two extra corn pones, and that'll do it."

Uncle Jesse put the meat on to boil and sat down and crossed his legs and took another swallow of coffee, and then lit his pipe. "How you aim to catch it?"

Skeeter crossed his legs too and leaned back in his chair, balancing the chair on its hind legs as the old man so often did. "It's a dog. And a dog goes with a man."

"That's right. A dog goes with a man."

"Heard you say so many a time. That a dog goes

74

with a man. Cat goes with a place. But a dog with a man."

"Maybe you aim to whistle it up."

"No, sir. I aim to take that food out in the swamp and just wait. I got a feeling that thing wants us as much as I want it."

Uncle Jesse took his pipe out of his mouth and looked into the bowl. It was clogged up as usual and he cleaned it out and filled it again. "You want my gun?" It took him a long time to say it.

"If you don't mind."

"You know how to tote it. Safety on. Keep it pointed toward the ground—"

"And don't climb a fence with it loaded." Skeeter had heard the instructions many times but never before had he gone out alone with the gun.

"What time you aiming to go?" Uncle Jesse broke a match between his fingers and did not look at the boy, for he could not.

"About daybust."

"And by yourself. Aim to go out by yourself."

"Yes, sir."

Uncle Jesse glanced over his shoulder toward the stove and the meat was boiling. "Mix them two extra pones with the meat and it'll go good. That thing mor'n likely is hungry for some good food."

"That's how I figure it," Skeeter said.

"You'll be careful. Like you said all along, that's a dog. But it's wild. You won't take no chances, now, boy?"

"I'll have your gun."

Uncle Jesse knocked the ashes out of his pipe and some burning tobacco fell on the floor and he stepped on it. Still he could not bring himself to look at the boy and felt his watery old eyes smarting in the lamplight. He tilted back his chair and reached for a cup and a saucer and put them before the boy and then lifted the coffeepot and filled the cup about half full. "Want a little coffee?"

"I'd like a little coffee." The boy measured his words as slowly as the old man measured the coffee.

"Pour in a little cream." Uncle Jesse pushed the can of milk across the table.

"You drink yours black."

"That's different. Pour a little cream in yours."

Skeeter tilted the can and stirred the milk into his cup and then poured the coffee into his saucer and blew on it and tasted it. It was very bitter. "Pretty good coffee," he said. He crossed his legs again and took another swallow. "Yes, sir, that's pretty good coffee."

CHAPTER ∼ ∼ ∼ ∼ FOUR

The boy woke up a long time before daybust and for a few minutes he lay there, snug in the cloud world between sun and shadows, and then he remembered that this was the day and he sat upright and his eyes popped open and he stared into the darkness, seeing nothing. He swung to the side of the bed and felt for his trousers and for his shirt and then he was dressed.

Uncle Jesse was breathing a medley of snores and rhythm and the boy peered across the room and could not see him because the cabin was in darkness and the night was heavy upon the swamp, holding it with sticky damp fingers. And this terrible thought came to the boy: Uncle Jesse might sleep for another hour and he must sit there and wait; just wait.

He wished the wind would rattle a window or that
a mouse would fiddle around the pots and pans, even a
big schooner bug—anything to wake up Uncle Jesse. But
there was no wind and the mice were sleeping.

He wished he could sneeze a pure D genuine sneeze.
Uncle Jesse would spot a play-like sneeze. Even a play-
like cough. He dared not scrape a chair. So he sat on
the side of the bed and froze his stare across the room
as though his stare and the wish would wake up Uncle
Jesse and they both could be up and about the big thing
that Skeeter had planned for this day.

Uncle Jesse's breathing leveled off to a steady rising
and falling and Skeeter flounced on the bed and
crawled across to the window and looked up at the element, as he called the sky. Nothing was stirring and
the darkness was mist-heavy and clammy. Then a bird
chirped to the east and another answered to the south.
A breeze wiggled a leaf on the tree by the window and
then the breeze died and all was still again.

Skeeter rested his chin on the window sill and was
dejected by the slowness of time.

"Can't hurry morn gloam." Uncle Jesse's voice filled
the room and yet it was not loud.

"Oh!" The boy turned from the window. "Uncle
Jesse?"

The old man grunted and flopped to his side.

"You awake? Didn't know you were awake."

Uncle Jesse reached out and fumbled for the lamp and lit it and the light danced across the floor and on the walls and then was steady. "Man can't sleep with a young'un squirming and scrounging around."

"Didn't go to wake you up." But he was glad and he jumped from his bed and went over to the stove and lifted an eye and peered in. "I'll get the fire going."

Uncle Jesse sat on the edge of his bed and yawned and stretched and scratched his chest and the backs of his hands and his head. "Don't waste no splinters. Gen'ly you take too many splinters to get a fire going."

"Wish we had a coal oil stove." Skeeter lit a rich pine splinter and put it on the grate and added more wood. He replaced the eye on the stove and twisted the damper. "Some day we'll get us a coal oil stove, huh, maybe, Uncle Jesse?"

"Mout'n." The old man pulled on his trousers and stood up and turned his back to the boy and pulled his nightgown over his head and slipped on his shirt. "Put a little water in the coffeepot. About a dipperful."

"Need mor'n a dipper. Sort of aiming on having me a good hot cup of coffee this morning; being's I'm going out."

"One dipper," Uncle Jesse said.

Skeeter did not argue but went to the porch and got

the water and poured it into the coffeepot and Uncle
Jesse watched him. "Little bit more won't hurt. Make
it two, three dippers. May want couple of cups myself;
getting up early like this."

The boy put in three dippers of water and took the
smallest eye off the stove and put the coffeepot directly
over the flame. He had seen Uncle Jesse do it so many
times and he did it just like him. The old man reached
for the skillet and Skeeter said, "I'll fix everything."

Without a word, Uncle Jesse went over to the table
and sat down and leaned back in his chair and the
yellow light of the lamp was in his eyes and he closed
his eyes and nodded his head slowly.

The boy cut the rind off a slab of bacon because
Uncle Jesse could not chew the rind and put the meat
in the pan. He broke four eggs into a bowl and beat
them and put the bowl aside and set the table and put
an empty cup by the old man's place and none by his
own. The bacon was ready and he removed it and
cooked the eggs in the grease. He sliced bread and
breakfast was ready.

He poured Uncle Jesse's coffee and the old man
emptied some in his saucer and blew on it and watched
the boy over the rim of the saucer. Skeeter crunched
his bacon and sopped his bread in the grease on his
plate and Uncle Jesse slurped his coffee, never taking

his eyes from the face of the boy. Then he scraped back his chair and walked over to the shelf and got a coffee cup and a saucer and wiped the saucer on his sleeve and put the cup and saucer by the boy's plate. Skeeter kept on eating and Uncle Jesse reached for the coffeepot and filled the cup half full and he went back to his chair and sat down.

"Smells good." The boy raised the cup to his lips.

"Put some cream in."

Skeeter tilted the can of condensed milk and spilled a few drops into his coffee.

"Ain't enough," Uncle Jesse said.

"Want it should be about half and half, maybe?"

" 'Bout that."

The boy did as he was told and weakened the coffee and drank it. He did not like it but he drank it all and tilted back his chair and patted his belly. "Nothing like a good cup of coffee and it coming daybust."

The old man filled his pipe and rolled a piece of paper into a taper and stuck the taper into the lamp and lit it and then his pipe. "Morn gloam be here t'reckly. When you going out?"

"Soon she shows grey."

"Where you reckon you'll be mostly?"

"Around the spring."

"Watch out for snakes."

"I'll be watching."

"Don't take no chances with that thing."

"Just a dog."

"Dogs go mad. And be they mad they'll jump you."

"I'll be watching."

Uncle Jesse puffed his pipe and the boy was silent and watched toward the east where the dawn grey soon must show.

"That gun's a single barrel," Uncle Jesse said. "Won't get but one shot."

"Ain't aiming to shoot."

"But if you have to, then don't miss."

"Ain't aiming to. Ain't aiming to shoot, but if I have to then I ain't aiming to miss."

"If you need me, holler. I'll be round and about."

"Won't need you."

"If you have to shoot and happen to miss, then grab yourself a stick. And start hollering. Don't try to run. Don't turn your back on that thing."

The boy nodded and began stacking the dishes.

"I'll do that," the old man said. "Clean 'em up after you're gone." He put his pipe on the table and got down the shotgun and handed it to the boy. "By time you're ready, it'll be time to go."

Skeeter broke the gun and pointed it toward the lamp and peered into the barrel and it was clean. "How many shells you figure I ought to take?"

"Three, four. Mout as well be set." The old man reached for his box of shells and handed five to the boy and Skeeter put them in his pocket. Then he went to the shelf and took down a lard can. In it were a few nails and some washers and a broken screwdriver. He emptied these into a sack and washed out the lard can and put in the food they had cooked the night before. He opened the back door and took down a frayed cotton rope that was hanging there.

The dawn breeze had come and birds were scolding and fussing around and the east was a dirty grey and then quickly a reddish glow and the night ran away and the shadows slunk into the trees that made them.

"How the element look?" Uncle Jesse asked.

The boy glanced at the sky. It was mottled and speckled. "Rain seed up there."

"Ain't going to rain." Uncle Jesse opened the front door and breathed deeply. "Mighty fine day. One of the good Lord's best, I reckon. He worked hard on this one. Tuckered Hisself out, maybe, but made it just right."

Skeeter stood in the doorway by the old man and the coiled rope was over his left shoulder and the lard bucket was in his left hand and the shotgun was in the crook of his right arm. He set the bucket on the porch and put a shell in the gun and clicked on the safety. "I'll be going."

"I'll be round and about."

The boy moved to the front steps and there he stopped and looked toward the river and then back at the old man. "Aim to get that thing, Uncle Jesse. Even do I go so far back in that swamp that I have to keep wiping at the shadows, I aim to get it."

"Like I said, I'll be round and about."

Skeeter walked down the path and Uncle Jesse leaned against the door and watched him swinging along. "Takes after his mamma, thank the good Lord. Takes after my folks. Got his papa's head and walks like his papa too. But he takes after my side of the family."

He watched until Skeeter was out of sight and turned back into the cabin and picked up his pipe. He blew out the lamp for the day was fullborn and then he glanced at the dirty dishes and left them there, and stepped to the back door and stared at the wood to be cut and he sat down on the back steps and watched the day unfold.

Skeeter stayed close to the path and the soft earth was between his bare toes. The mist, rising fast, clung to his eyelashes and curled his long hair. As soon as he was beyond Uncle Jesse's sight he clicked off the safety on the gun and hunched his shoulders and was a hunter

stalking game. Like Uncle Jesse. No, he was with
Stonewall Jackson; with Nathan Bedford Forrest. Were
there ever any others?

His finger was on the trigger guard and the gun was
pointed at the ground before him. There might be a
snake under the next log or a rabbit behind the next
bush. But there was nothing, only birds chattering at
him and then flying away.

He slipped out of the path and crept behind a clump
of briars and peered toward the river that was gliding
yellow and immensely silent, and the mist hugging the
river and then swirling high into the trees. He moved
from behind the briars and toward the spring and felt
for the breeze and it was drifting his way. That was
good.

He still could not see the spring and the first sound
he heard was a heavy grunt. Might be a bear and if a
bear were at the spring then nothing else would be
there, for all things feared the swamp bears. Even the
alligators slunk away from the bears and the catamounts
climbed high.

The boy swallowed hard and crouched again and
moved on. He would aim at that bear's head. That was
the place to kill a bear. Slap-dab in the head. Dead sure
between the eyes. Pull the gun tight against the shoulder
and draw a bead and squeeze the trigger. Never jerk it.

The gun butt hard to the shoulder and a quick sure bead and then fire. He would fire and break the gun and load quickly and be ready for his second shot. This one to the chest.

He cut back to the path because somehow the path seemed safer and then he saw the spring and the wild pigs wallowing in the muddy trough between the spring and the river. He laughed at himself. Bear, my hind foot. Nothing but a bunch of swamp pigs messing around and rooting for food. He picked up a clod and chunked at them and they grunted and walked away.

The water from the overflow had backed into the spring and it was so muddy that even the mellowbugs were in hiding and Skeeter looked at all the tracks thereabout and most of them were pig tracks, although a deer had been that way and a coon or so. The sun was high enough for its warmth to tingle his skin and crisp his long hair at the back of his neck, and the mist was burning away.

He laid the gun across a log and was very careful about this, and sat down by the spring to wait; and the swamp woke up while he sat there. The sun turned the river from yellow to muddy brown and the swamp buzzed and hummed and hissed as the day things went forth for food. The spring ran clear and he waited until it was clear enough to see the bottom and the minnows and grasses there, and then he drank. The mellowbugs came out of hiding. A water spider skipped across and dragonflies hovered close. The pigs were out of sight and if any other animals were coming for water they soon would come, for the day was full open.

Skeeter took the food out of the lard can and put a piece of meat on a tuft of grass and another piece in the path. He closed the bucket and buried his face in the water again and took a deep pull and wiped his face on his sleeve. He picked up the gun and the rope and the lard bucket and walked toward the river, circling the spring until he found the spot he wanted: a tangle of weeds and vines between him and the spring and a log to sit on and a tree for shade.

Now there was nothing to do but wait. At first he was very still as a hunter should be, as Uncle Jesse was when he was hunting. Then a parade of ants passed near his foot and he jerked his foot and showered them with dirt. He watched them scamper and reform the line and march away.

Again he was still, listening. It lasted maybe a minute and he squirmed and teased a piece of bark off of the tree and began chewing it. A squirrel poked his nose over a branch and peered at him and hurried away. A butterfly flitted in and floated off. Gnats were whining around his ears and mosquitoes hunched on his hands and ankles and he brushed them off. He was lonely and time was so slow and he started humming to keep himself company:

"Went to the river and couldn't get across
So I paid five dollars for an old grey hoss—"

He had forgot the words and so he whistled the song, whistling with his tongue against his teeth, and then the whistle was a gasp; for standing there between him and the river and within chunking distance was the thing, its head cocked to one side and staring at him, its smooth tail curved high over its back.

The boy forgot the gun and the rope and everything. He just looked. Then he instinctively held out his hand and was not afraid. He got up from the log and took a step or two and squatted and snapped his fingers and whistled softly. The animal cocked its head to the other side and backed away.

"You ain't nothing but a little old dog. Why don't you come here?"

He patted the ground and held out his hand again.

The strange creature tilted its nose and sniffed.

"How come you didn't eat that meat? How come you slipping up on me like this? You ain't nothing but a little old dog. A little old girl dog."

The animal drooped its nose and Skeeter saw it as

88

plain as day and it was about as high as his knees. The little wrinkled face was almost sad and the white hair blazed down the chest and around the throat, but mostly the thing was red and the hair very short.

"Ain't going to hurt you. Wouldn't hurt you for nothing."

The dog, for she was a dog, blinked her eyes and was trembling but did not run away. Slowly the boy walked toward her holding out his hand and talking to her and then he knelt by her and stroked her and she stopped trembling. She kept blinking her eyes that were hazel, and sniffed his hands and his feet. A pleading look of bewilderment and hope came to her eyes and she fastened them on Skeeter, wistfully at first and then quizzically. And her eyes filled up.

"She's crying. Be John dog if she ain't crying." Skeeter was crying too. "Never saw no dog that could cry before." He pulled her to him and she turned over and Skeeter scratched her, and the tears went out of her eyes and she closed them, and stretched. Then she chuckled, a happy mixture of chortle and yodel.

"Now you're laughing." The boy held her close. "Ain't no dog due to laugh and cry. Like Uncle Jesse said, it ain't natural." But he, too, was laughing.

Skeeter lifted her in his arms and lugged her back to the log where he had left the rope and he fastened the rope around her neck and tied a knot that would have held a buffalo. He reached into the lard can and took out the rest of the food and fed her from his hand. Then he slipped the handle of the can over his arm and picked up the gun. "Come on. Let's go home. Me and you."

The dog followed willingly and the rope was not necessary at all, but Skeeter was taking no chances. They went back to the spring and the food that he had left there was gone. "You slipped in and ate it." He knelt by the dog and squeezed her head between his hands and played with her. "You fooled me. Didn't know you were anywhere nigh and here you were round and about all the time." He put his cheek against her head and she chuckled.

He wrapped the rope around his wrist and they headed up the path and when the cabin was in sight Skeeter began running, and the dog was at his heels. "Uncle Jesse!" He shouted the greeting and the news. "I got it."

The old man still was sitting on the back steps, staring at the saw that should have been running and the wood that should have been cut, and when he heard the boy he moved faster than he had moved in many years and jogged around the corner of the cabin.

"I got it. Told you I'd get it," Skeeter yelled.

90

"Well, now, I do know." Uncle Jesse was flabber-gasted and looked hard at the strange animal. "That ain't nothing but a little old dog."

"Little old girl dog."

"Well, now, I do declare." Uncle Jesse moved toward the boy and the dog leaped between him and Skeeter and braced herself.

"Hold that thing." The old man stepped back. "Ain't rightly friendly."

Skeeter tightened the rope and slipped his arm around the dog's chest. "That's just Uncle Jesse. Lives around here, too. Just Uncle Jesse."

The dog looked from the boy to the old man, and the old man still was skeptical and kept his distance. "Didn't growl or nothing. Just jumped."

"Can't growl," Skeeter said. "Do she ought to be barking or growling she just laughs."

"Do tell."

"It's so." He handed the gun and the bucket to Uncle Jesse and snapped his fingers and whistled and the dog followed him around the cabin, and Uncle Jesse followed both of them, shuffling along and muttering his amazement.

Skeeter glanced at the uncut wood and said nothing and went over and sat on the back steps and the dog sat at his feet and never took her eyes from his face.

"She's mine, Uncle Jesse. I found her."

"Wonder how she got around here?" The old man propped against the cabin and studied the animal.

"Don't know, but she's mine."

"That dog's been around folks. Belongs to somebody."

"Belongs to me. I found her."

"Nobody around here ever had a dog like that. Laughing when it oughta bark. That's a furrin' dog, or something."

"Maybe it's a Yankee dog. You know how funny Yankees are."

"Don't know about Yankees, thank the good Lord. But that dog's been around folks and don't belong around here."

"Does now." There was defiance in the boy's words. "Got me a dog, Uncle Jesse."

"Sure have. Got yourself a dog all right. What you aim to call her?"

"Ain't thought about it. Maybe Dixie. How that sound? Dixie."

"Not much." Uncle Jesse inched closer to the steps and held out his hand and the dog paid him no mind and rubbed against Skeeter's leg. The old man's lips tightened into a pout. "Half the dogs in this swamp named Dixie."

"Then how about Pal?"

"Nothing to brag about. All the dogs that ain't named Dixie are named Pal." He moved even closer and sat down by the boy and pretended to ignore the dog. "She's yours, and you got a right to call her what you want to. But if I had a dog like her, I'd give her a *real* name. Som'n that means som'n."

"Then how about Tray?" Skeeter said it quickly remembering something.

"How come you think of Tray? Used to know a song about a dog named Tray. *Ol' Dog Tray*. Be John Brown. How come you think of Tray?"

"You used to sing that song to me when I was a little bitty boy. That's how come."

"Well, now, I do declare. So you remember that?" He looked away from the boy and the dog and into summer's blue haze. "Fair to middlin' name, but it's for a boy dog. Course, I don't want to butt in. You found her and she's yours. Don't even like me."

"Just don't know you yet. And I want that you should help me name her."

"Then how about Gertrude?"

"Gertrude?"

"Uh huh. That's a pretty name."

"Don't think much of it myself."

"Reckoned you wouldn't." The old man held out his

93

hand again and touched the dog and she licked his hand. "Know'd a lady named Gertrude once. Way back before you got here. Your mamma know'd her, too. She had pensy eyes and was as pure as the jest of God. Punied up and died a long time ago."

"We'll name her Gertrude," Skeeter said quickly and understood more than he had been told.

"Not unless you want to." He was stroking the dog. "But this here dog is a lady like Gertrude was. Keeps herself clean as a coon and don't even smell like a dog. She's a pure D lady, to who laid a chunk."

"Then let's call her Lady? How that sound—Lady?"

"You got it." The old man slapped his knee in approval. "Now that's a name what is a name. Huh, Lady? Ain't it, Lady?" He sat on the ground beside the dog and ran his hand down her back and around her curved tail and down her legs, feeling the muscles.

Skeeter got on the ground, too, and did exactly as the old man had done. "We got us a dog, ain't we, Uncle Jesse? Ain't we, Lady?"

Lady looked from the boy to the old man and licked their hands and chuckled.

"Take off the rope," Uncle Jesse said. "This dog ain't going nowhere."

"Ain't sure."

94

"I am. Wild mules couldn't pull this dog away from here."

Skeeter loosened the rope and slipped it over Lady's head and she ran around the back yard and came back to his side and then followed the boy and the old man into the cabin.

Uncle Jesse crumbled corn bread in a plate and wet it with pot likker and put it before her. She sniffed the food disdainfully at first and ate it only when she saw the boy fix a bowl for himself and for the old man. She licked herself clean and explored the cabin and sniffed the brush broom and the hickory nuts and then the beds, and jumped on Skeeter's bed and tucked her nose under her paws and went to sleep.

"Acts like she owns the place," Skeeter said. "And like you said, she's been around folks. Reckon she's a hunting dog, Uncle Jesse?"

"How she going to hunt if she can't bark? How she going to tree?"

"Maybe she's a bird dog. Bird dogs don't have to bark."

"Maybe." The old man stacked the empty bowls and stood in the back doorway and looked at the woodpile, then over at the boy and at the sleeping dog. "Let's walk around some and see how she does. Evening's just starting."

Skeeter was hoping for this and he whistled to the dog and she raised her head and then he called her and she came to him. "Knows her name already."

"Knows you." Uncle Jesse walked out of the cabin and the boy was right behind him and Lady was there, too.

They headed toward the east, toward the ridges that rimmed the swamp and to the dry land beyond, and had gone about a mile before Uncle Jesse spoke. "She follows good." He turned to the dog and commanded, "Heel!"

Lady cocked her head and turned to the boy and chuckled. It was obvious that she'd never heard the order before.

"Ain't been trained," Skeeter said. "That's sure as shooting. Maybe she ain't no bird dog."

"Maybe she don't understand us, being from outside. Wave her off and see what she does."

The boy patted her head and waved his right arm in a wide circle, the signal that she should range and cast. She sat on her haunches and looked at him. Skeeter whistled and signaled again and still she did not move. "Get going, Lady," he ordered.

Uncle Jesse shook his head. "Ain't no bird dog. Hate to tell you, but it's so."

They walked across a ridge and came to a wilderness

of broom straw circled by pines and Uncle Jesse noticed her first. Her nose came up and into the breeze and she wheeled.

He caught the boy's eye and they both were motionless and then Lady's curved tail suddenly was still and her head was poised.

"Flash pointing," Jesse said.

Lady held the strange point for only a second and then dashed toward a patch of wiregrass about 60 yards away. Halfway there, she broke her gait and began creeping. A whirr of feathers sounded in the wiregrass and a covey of quail exploded almost under her nose. She sprang for a bird and missed it.

"Partridge!" Jesse's mouth sagged open and his Adam's apple bobbed up and down.

Skeeter was trembling and his face was white. "Look how far she smelled them birds. And she pointed."

"Flash pointed. Any dog will flash point."

Skeeter whistled and Lady came to him and sat at his feet and ran out her tongue and panted.

"She'll hunt birds, Uncle Jesse. I can train her."

"She'll flush." He walked on and often glanced back at the boy and the dog to see how they were doing and Lady stayed at Skeeter's heels and made no effort to range or hunt.

They circled the ridges and came back to the swamp

and the afternoon was almost gone when they got to the river. "Tell you what," Uncle Jesse said. "Let's cross over and let Gates Watson see that dog."

"How come?" the boy asked quickly.

"Gates might know what kind of dog she is and where she came from. Gates knows a heap."

"I'm sort of tuckered," the boy protested. "We ought to head for home. Besides, Gates don't know ever'thing."

"Maybe you're right." Uncle Jesse didn't press the point. "It's coming evening gloam and like you said we maybe ought to go home." He struck off through the swamp without another word.

The twilight had faded when they reached the cabin and Uncle Jesse said not a word but began fixing supper while Skeeter sat on the front steps and held his dog close to him and watched the night creep into the swamp.

"Better come eat," Uncle Jesse called.

He did and there was a plate of food by his chair for Lady. Supper was over and the dishes were cleaned before Skeeter spoke a word. "Reckon Gates mout know what kind of dog I got?"

"Mout'n. You know how smart Gates is. All them books and things."

98

"But you reckon he mout know who used to own my dog?"

"Ain't saying. It's your business."

The boy propped his elbows on the table and stared into the lamplight, at the insects swarming there and dying. "You know, I don't aim to tell Gates about my dog."

"Your business."

"Ain't Gates that's bothering me. It's Mister Cash. He's bound to find out."

"Bound to." Uncle Jesse took off his shoes and lit his pipe and reached out his bare foot and scratched the dog with his long toes.

"If anybody knows who she used to belong to, it'll be Mister Cash."

"Mor'n likely."

The boy looked away from the lamp and toward the window and into the swamp beyond, the trees tall in the moonlight and the night things crying. "Don't mean to be uppity, Uncle Jesse. Don't mean to try to sit in the big chair and do any big talking. But I'm telling you: I don't aim for nobody to take my dog. I found her, and she's mine."

Old Jesse Jackson grunted and went to the porch and got a dipper of water and brought it to the dog and knelt beside her while she drank it.

"You heard me, didn't you? Ain't nobody going to take my dog."

"Ain't nobody going to take your dog." Uncle Jesse picked up his shoes and put them by the side of his bed. "Let's get some sleep. Got to cut that wood tomorrow. Just got to."

Skeeter went to his own bed and Lady followed him and when he was bedded down she lay at his feet. Uncle Jesse blew out the lamp and the cabin was in darkness and soon the old man was asleep and dreamed of his store-bought teeth and all the roasting ears he would eat. And then Skeeter was asleep and dreamed that he and Lady were in the broom straw hunting birds; and he had a .20 gauge shotgun.

There is no way of knowing if Lady dreamed or not. But once she chuckled in her sleep and snuggled closer to the boy.

CHAPTER ∽ ∽ ∽ ∽ FIVE

WITH ANOTHER MOUTH TO FEED, UNCLE JESSE BEAT the sun up and had been at the woodpile about an hour when Skeeter appeared in the back doorway. His hair was tangled into a snarl and he kept yawning as he stood there and watched Lady sniff around the cabin.

The old man scarcely glanced up. "Breakfast on the stove." He yelled it above the whine of the saw.

"Seen it," Skeeter yelled back. "Just wondering about a cup of coffee. Sort of figured on having me a good cup of coffee this morning."

Uncle Jesse did not reply, just grunted and the boy knew that the answer was "no," and so he turned back into the cabin. The old man toned down the saw and watched him moving around the stove and then he

101

yelled again: "Go wash your face. And comb that hair."

Skeeter did as he was told and Uncle Jesse went back to his work, muttering to himself. "Got to cut that boy's hair. One of these days I'm going to do it if it's the last thing I do. Got to watch his hair and manners. Sprouting up fast, that young'un is."

The day was getting hot and so was the old man when Skeeter and Lady came out to the woodpile and stood around and watched Uncle Jesse work. The sawdust was flying and some of it stuck to the old man's sweaty face and some of it got down his collar and around his neck and itched. "Aim to stand there all day?" Uncle Jesse had his habits on and was in a bad humor. He always was when he had to work. "Maybe your back's broke, or som'n."

Lady sat on the ground and ran out her tongue as though jeering at him and Skeeter went over and began stacking the wood. Uncle Jesse was ashamed of himself. He eased off the motor and let it idle and pressed his hands into the small of his back and stretched. Then he squatted and patted Lady and spoke to Skeeter: "Have enough breakfast?"

"Plenty. And I'll saw awhile and you rest."

"Ain't tired. Besides, you got to go over to the Watsons. Buttermilk day. We plum' out."

"Yes, sir. I know it. Might as well go on over there

before it gets too hot."

"Mout as well. I'll keep cutting."

"Think I'll leave my dog here."

"She'll follow you. Can't be watching her, and me cutting."

"Then I'll tie her up."

"She's your dog." The old man turned to the motor and soon it was racing again and the saw whining and the sawdust flying.

Skeeter went into the cabin and got two buckets and the frayed rope and called Lady to the shade of a water oak and tied her and started away, but she strained against the rope and choked herself.

"Won't stay tied," the boy called to Uncle Jesse.

"Is that a fact?"

"Maybe you could keep your eye on her."

"Got wood to cut like I told you."

"Then I'll take her with me." He was hoping Uncle Jesse would come up with an idea and at least volunteer to keep Lady there with him, but the old man kept feeding wood to the saw and had nothing to say.

"I said then I'd have to take her with me." Skeeter raised his voice to be sure Uncle Jesse heard him above the noise of the saw.

"She's your dog."

The boy felt put upon and unloved and snatched the

rope off of his dog and coiled it and put it over his shoulder. He picked up the two buckets and whistled for Lady to follow him and struck off toward the river beyond which lived the Watson family. The whine of the saw grew faint and he was out of sight of the cabin and was mad at Uncle Jesse and wished that he was grown and his own boss.

He cut north through the swamp and toward the little bayou where they kept their skiff. They were at the edge of a canebrake when Lady's nose tilted and she braced to a point. However, she held it only for a few seconds and darted to the bayou and dived into a clump of reeds and snatched a water rat. She was eating it when Skeeter ran up.

"Don't do that!" He grabbed one of her ears and shook her head and scolded her. "Ain't you got good sense? Don't run into water after things. Snake or a gator'll grab you."

Lady dropped the rat and tucked her head and when she looked up at him her eyes were filled and that woeful expression was on her face. Skeeter tried to explain. "Didn't go to hurt your feelings." He knelt by her. "Just doing it for your own good. Just don't want you to get killed."

Her eyes cleared as she accepted his apology and licked his face and they walked on down the bayou to the skiff that was tied to a root, and they got in it and Skeeter paddled down the bayou and into the river and then across it while his dog sat in the bow and chuckled that haunting laugh that sounded like a yodel and ended in that weird "gro-o-o."

On the other side of the river, Skeeter knew that the time and place of decision was upon him and he tied the skiff and called his dog to his side. "Now, you're going to stay here and wait for me."

Lady cocked her head impudently.

"Be gone thirty, maybe forty minutes. Over yonder across the ridge. You ain't going."

He got the rope from the skiff and tied her and petted her until she lay down and then he picked up the buckets and started away. She sprang to her feet and strained at the rope and he turned and cuffed her. "Lay down! Stay right here."

That pitiful, pleading look was on her face and her eyes filled. It wrenched his heart, but he cuffed her again and spoke sternly, "None of that bawling, neither."

The boy meant business and she knew that he meant business and she lay still and watched him move off and he turned only once to look back at her. "Stay there, Lady. Like I'm telling you, stay right there."

She did, and now she knew that the boy was her master, and she liked it.

He hurried out of the swamp and across the ridge where the Watsons lived in a five room house that had running water and a coal oil stove. They farmed about sixty acres and grew corn and sweet potatoes. Their pigs ran wild in the swamp and they had three milk cows. Ed Watson was head of the family and folks called him Uncle Ed and called his wife Aunt Bonnie Dew or sometimes just Aunt Bonnie. She was born over in Louisiana where they spoke a lot of French and had been christened Bon Dieu, but somehow the swamp folks twisted it into Bonnie Dew and she didn't mind at all. She and Uncle Ed had a raft of children and Gates Watson was the oldest and was the only fellow thereabouts who had been away to college.

Some of the Watson children saw Skeeter coming and ran out to meet him and escorted him to their house where Aunt Bonnie Dew was waiting on the porch. She was a tall, bony woman whose shoes were always run over. She had been sweeping the porch and she beat the broom against the steps to dislodge the dirt and called out to Skeeter: " 'Bout time you got here. Come on in and visit awhile."

"Ain't got long," the boy said. "I'll get my buttermilk and head on back, thanking you just the same."

Aunt Bonnie Dew propped her broom against the wall and commanded her brood to scatter and they did, and then she studied Skeeter and shook her head in disapproval. "How come Jesse Jackson don't cut your hair?"

"Aims to one of these days." The boy had reached the steps and he put the buckets on the porch.

"Come on in the house. Got a pitcher of sweet milk just waiting. Boy like you needs sweet milk. Jesse Jackson ought to be shot for not feeding you sweet milk."

"Don't like sweet milk." Skeeter immediately defended Uncle Jesse. "Like coffee myself."

"Coffee! You standing there telling me that Jesse Jackson lets a young'un like you drink coffee?"

"All I want. Had me a good cup of coffee just before I left the house. No cream, neither."

Aunt Bonnie Dew was indignant. "Coffee will make a young'un turn brown and give him the jaundice." She herself was as black as ebony. "Besides, it'll salivate you, like calomel. And all your teeth'll fall out. Like your Uncle Jesse. He mor'n likely got salivated when he was a young'un. He ought to be shot with a washtub." She snatched up the buckets and started inside.

"Where's Gates?"

"Out back som'rs. You ask him about coffee." She opened the screen door on which a wad of cotton was tied to keep off the flies, and disappeared into the house, mumbling to herself, "Jesse Jackson ain't worth the salt it takes to feed him. Too lazy to fan flies."

The boy walked around to the back and saw Gates down by the barn and moseyed on down that way. Gates was tinkering with a gasoline motor that pumped water into the house. He looked up and nodded solemnly. "Howdy, Claude."

"Howdy, Gates. How you been?"

"Pretty good. And you?"

"Pretty good." Skeeter stepped to the shed and got a bucket and turned it upside down and sat on it.

Gates wiped his hands on a rag and looked closely at the boy and then up toward the house and over toward the ridge. "Come by yourself?"

"Uh huh."

"Everything all right at your place?"

"Pretty good." Skeeter leaned over and examined the motor. Wished they had a gasoline motor to pump water. Then he wouldn't have to go to the spring so often.

Gates took the plunger out of the motor and dipped it in coal oil and wiped it clean. He was deliberate in his motions and then he said, "What's eating you, Claude?"

"Nothing much. Me and Uncle Jesse got to talking about dogs last night. Know anything about dogs?"

"Maybe. What's on your mind?"

"Uncle Jesse said that almost any dog could be trained to hunt birds. Cep'n feists and dogs like that. I said that only bird dogs could hunt birds."

Gates held the plunger up to the sun and wiped away the last bit of grime. "I'm on your Uncle Jesse's side. I believe almost any dog can be taught to hunt birds. Of course, not as good as a bird dog. But good enough. A dog is pretty smart."

"About the smartest animal there is, I reckon. Coming and going." Skeeter locked his hands around his knee and leaned back as he had seen Uncle Jesse do so often.

Gates put the plunger back in the motor. "I read somewhere that an elephant is the smartest animal there is. That an elephant is up near the top and a horse is down near the bottom. Mule's got more sense than a horse."

"How 'bout a dog? Where he stand?"

"Up near the top. You can train a dog to do most anything." He pulled the motor closer to him and took out the bearings. "Except maybe laugh and cry and things like that, like talking." He didn't look up, but kept his eyes hard on his work.

Quickly, Skeeter changed the trend of the talk. "Heard Uncle Jesse say that a pig is about the smartest animal there is." He reached down and got a clod and crumbled it in his hands. "Uncle Jesse says he seen a pig that was trained to hunt birds."

Gates nodded slowly. "That's right. Over in Alabama, that was. A pig is mighty smart. Pigs and rats are about the smartest animals we have around here. They look after themselves. They make it."

"If a pig can be trained to hunt birds, then most any dog can. That's what Uncle Jesse said."

"He said right."

The boy got to his feet and picked up the bucket and tossed it back into the shed. "I'll be going. I'll tell Uncle Jesse you said he was right—that most any dog can be trained to hunt birds. Just a little talk me and Uncle Jesse had. No words or hard feelings. Just talk. You know how it goes."

"I know. Drop by any time you're over this way."

"Much obliged. Hope the motor works all right."

"It will."

Skeeter hesitated, then said, "Just happen to think about it—you been hearing anything funny over in the swamp? Like a h'ant laughing?"

Gates raised his head and looked the boy squarely in the eyes. "Not a thing."

"Heard anything about anybody losing a dog, or something?"

Gates never took his eyes from his friend's face. "I haven't heard a thing, Claude. Don't let it bother you."

Then it was that Skeeter wondered if Gates already knew about the dog. Funny about colored folks—how they know things sometimes even before they happen. It had been only a day since he had found Lady and nobody had been by the cabin, and yet Gates might know. But if he knew of anybody who had lost a dog or something like that, then surely he would tell his friend. On the other hand, funny how shut-mouth colored folks can be—even to friends.

Skeeter went back to the house and Aunt Bonnie Dew was waiting on the front porch. The two buckets of buttermilk were on the steps and there was a third bucket, and Skeeter knew what was in it. Nevertheless, he opened the top and peeped in to be polite. It was filled with cold biscuits, big fat brown ones, and baked sweet potatoes. "Thank you." He replaced the top. "Me and Uncle Jesse both thank you. You make the best biscuits I ever et."

"Stick a stick through the handles and tote 'em over your shoulder." Aunt Bonnie Dew found herself wishing she had the white boy in her care. She'd fatten him on sweet milk and trim his hair, and Gates would make him go to school, maybe off to college like Gates had done.

Skeeter looked under the porch and found a stick and swung the buckets over his shoulder and walked away without haste, but when he reached the ridge and was beyond sight of the Watsons, he began running, and the buttermilk sloshed in the buckets.

Lady was right where he had left her. She had chewed

the rope in two and had freed herself, but was waiting for him.

He threw his arms around her and they rolled on the ground together and he was laughing. She chuckled, too, and he opened the bucket and gave her one of Aunt Bonnie Dew's biscuits. Then he patted the side of the skiff and she jumped in and he paddled back across the river and into the bayou and was careful to tie the boat.

"Going to make a bird dog out of you sure as the Lord made little apples." He held another of the biscuits high above her head and she jumped for it. "You got sense enough to hunt birds. But you can't hunt rats or coons or things like that. Hear me! They'll lead you into the river and trap you."

Lady sat on her haunches and ran out her tongue.

"I'll learn you not to mess with rats." He hunted around until he found the rat Lady had killed and then unraveled a bit of the rope and tied the rat around her neck. Lady was humiliated and tried to claw it off and, failing, her eyes overflowed with tears and Skeeter tapped her nose with the rat. "Stop that bawling. I aim to make you sick of rats. Come on."

She followed him and the dead rat dangled from her neck and against her chest.

He took the shortest way home and was walking along humming that old grey hoss song and any minute now he should hear the whine of the saw to tell him that Uncle Jesse still was hard at it. But he heard nothing, only the wind in the cypress and he looked down at Lady and she looked up at him and they quickened their pace. Then the cabin was in sight and all was still thereabouts, but Mister Cash's truck was parked near the front steps and that meant the storekeeper was nigh.

Skeeter's first impulse was to go back into the swamp and stay there until Mister Cash had gone and yet something told him that was not the thing to do. He couldn't hide his dog forever and, besides, Mister Cash was bound to find out sooner or later. So there was nothing to do but face up to it and get it over with.

He left the buckets on the front porch in the shade and went around the side of the cabin and Uncle Jesse and Mister Cash were out by the woodpile. Uncle Jesse was propped against the stacked wood and Mister Cash was squatting on the ground.

Uncle Jesse saw him first and then Mister Cash, and the storekeeper paid him no mind but gawked at Lady and then busted out laughing. The dog was at Skeeter's feet. Her tail was curved high and the dead rat and the frayed rope trailed from her neck. Uncle Jesse did not even smile, but Mister Cash slapped his leg and his little pot-belly shook his mirth. "So that's it! That's the thing that outrun my Gabe and jumped my hog dogs."

Skeeter felt his neck reddening and then his face and he stooped by his dog and untied the rat and threw it away. Be John Brown if he'd humiliate his dog in front of a man like Mister Cash. Only then did he speak and he strained for politeness. "Good morning, Mister Cash. How you like my dog?"

The storekeeper glanced at Uncle Jesse and walked over and patted Lady and she sniffed his hand and turned her head toward the truck and was tense and nervous. "It's a dog all right," Cash said. "Never saw one like it, but it's a dog. Rat runner, huh?"

Uncle Jesse shifted his position maybe an inch or two. He was comfortable there in the shade and leaning against the woodpile. "Cash drove up a few minutes back. Know'd he aim to stick around, so told him you'd caught that thing."

"But you didn't tell me much." Cash spoke over his shoulder and then squatted by Lady to examine her. "Never saw such shut-mouth folks about a dog. What you two up to? Aiming to hide her?"

"Can't hide a dog." Skeeter crossed the yard and stood by Uncle Jesse, and Lady came to him and stretched out in the shade.

"That's right," Cash said. "Looks like a pretty good dog."

"She does all right."

"Do she sure enough laugh?"

"Sort of chuckles. Cries, too."

"Beaten'st thing I ever heard of." Cash took off his felt hat and mopped his forehead. "What she good for? Rats?"

"Hunt anything," Skeeter said. "Aim to make a bird dog out of her, don't we, Uncle Jesse?"

"Maybe." The old man moved deeper into the shade and sat down and rested his back against the woodpile.

"Mister Cash—" Skeeter had to know and so he asked it forthrightly. "You know what kind of dog I found myself?"

"Ain't even beginning to about to know. Just know one thing—she don't belong around here."

"Then you don't know nobody who lost a dog?"

Cash tilted his hat low on his forehead and looked hard at Lady. "Ain't nobody around here lost that dog. But I know one thing. I know a boy who found hisself a dog."

"And finder's keepers, ain't she, Cash?" Uncle Jesse suggested.

"Finder's keepers. That's how things are around here." The storekeeper jerked his head at Jesse and the old man got reluctantly to his feet and walked from the shade into the sunshine and then Cash said, "Come on out to the truck. Got something to show both of you."

They headed for the truck and Lady ran before them and held her nose close to the ground and was excited. Cash climbed into the truck and opened a crate and out stepped the most beautiful dog that any of them had ever seen; an English setter with soft eyes and a cold nose and a majestic demeanor.

Uncle Jesse stepped back as though in the presence of a dignitary and he whistled softly and this was evidence of his admiration. Even Lady moved back, but kept her eyes on the setter, blinking slowly and bracing herself after she had retreated to the proper distance. It wasn't fear. It was respect.

Skeeter, however, stepped forward to be closer to the magnificent creature, and his eyes were wide in awe. He did not speak because he knew no adequate words and so he just stood by the truck and stared.

The setter raised his head high and Cash spoke to him and only then did his dog leap from the truck and go to him, ignoring everything else, even Lady.

Quickly, Skeeter called his dog and she passed close to the setter and was trembling. "She ain't scared," Skeeter said. Lady raised her nose to the big dog in a gesture of friendliness, but the setter was disdainful and looked up at Cash and then around at all of them, and down at Lady.

The boy walked over and caught his dog by the scruff

of the neck and pulled her away and squatted by her and stroked her. "Where you get that setter?" he asked. "That's a lot of dog."

The storekeeper grinned his pride. "This is a pure D English setter. This is a bird dog that is a bird dog. From way back."

"And you ain't stretching it." Uncle Jesse had to get in his comment. He had never seen such a dog before but, nevertheless, he had to nod his approval and pretend his knowledge. "Pretty a setter as I ever seen. Pure D English setter, all right."

Skeeter still was stroking Lady and she no longer was nervous. "Never saw a dog like that. Like I said, where did you get him?"

"Over in Alabama." Cash spoke to his dog and the setter leaped back onto the truck and posed there, looking around like a king. "Bought him over in Alabama a few weeks ago. Like I was telling Jesse before you got back—there could be some dogs as good as this one, but there ain't none better."

"Just found out about it this morning," Uncle Jesse said to Skeeter because he didn't want the boy to think he had been left out of anything. "Ol' Cash was rightly shut-mouth about it."

"Just didn't run off at the mouth," the storekeeper explained. "The man I bought him from brung him over last night." He opened the crate and the dog went in.

There was something about all of this that puzzled Skeeter, but he did not push for an explanation. That would be prying and unmannerable and, besides, he knew that the story would come out if he were patient. He had a feeling why Mister Cash had brought his dog out to the cabin, but he wasn't sure and so he approached the subject in a roundabout way. "Well, all I can say is that you've got yourself a bird dog. What's his name?"

"Millard Fillmore."

"Sir?"

"I said Millard Fillmore. That's his name."

Skeeter thought Mister Cash was funning with him and Uncle Jesse snorted his derision. "What you doing naming a good dog like that a crazy name like that? Trying to be funny?"

"Ever hear of Millard Fillmore?" Cash demanded.

"Naw." Uncle Jesse pushed his hat to the back of his head and walked around to the shade of the truck. "Been around here all my life and never heard no such name. For man, boy, dog, or goat. Horse or mule, neither."

The storekeeper scratched the fringe of hair over his ear and his eyes crinkled his merriment. "Millard Fillmore was president of the United States."

"Never heard of him," Uncle Jesse said. "Must not have 'mounted to much. Never heard of him."

"Nobody ever named nothing after Millard Fillmore," Cash said. "President of the United States and nobody ever named nothing after him."

"Aim to call your dog that?" Skeeter asked. He had never heard of President Fillmore either. They hadn't come to the presidents at school yet and if they had it was on some of the many days that he had missed. "Lot of name to call a dog."

"Going to call him Mill," Cash said. "Better name for calling. But he's registered as Millard Fillmore."

"Registered, huh?" Uncle Jesse was impressed. He had never seen a registered dog before.

"In the book. Got him in the book just like Yankees and them rich bird dog men over in Alabama and up around Atlanta and places like that." Cash opened the door to his truck and climbed behind the wheel and, for an instant, Skeeter thought he was going to get away without telling all the story.

"Ain't leaving, are you?" the boy asked.

"Uh huh. Your Uncle Jesse will tell you how come I drove out here with my dog."

Jesse Jackson came out of his slouch and out of the shade and stood tall in the sun. "Reckon you'll tell him, Cash."

"Reckon I will. It's my place to tell him." He rested his arms on the door of his truck and looked down at

Skeeter and at Lady. "Brought Mill out here for you and Jesse to look after him and work him for me."

"That's what I figured," Skeeter said. "Know'd you didn't aim to keep that dog around your store. He needs working."

Cash looked away toward the cabin and then the woods. "But you got a dog. Didn't know you'd found that dog when I came out."

"Got room for two dogs," the boy said hopefully. The storekeeper would pay well for them to keep his dog and work him. Then, too, such a fine bird dog would be the very thing for Lady. The setter could teach her how to hunt. "I'd feed him good and take him to the woods every day."

"No. I reckon not."

"It ain't on account of my dog, is it?"

"Now, I ain't saying that."

"He ain't said that, Skeeter," Uncle Jesse broke in.

"But you don't want your dog running with mine." The boy spoke slowly and there was a trace of bitterness, even anger, in his words.

"Ain't saying that at all." Cash avoided the boy's eyes.

"Why don't you come right out and say it, Mister Cash. That my dog ain't good enough to run with yours."

"Now you acting like I low-rated your dog. And I ain't. Just that Mill's a fine bird dog and ain't no telling what yours is. She hunts rats. If my dog run with yours, he mor'n likely would learn bad habits. Like rat hunting. Or maybe coons and rabbits, and things like that." Cash chewed the words as though he disliked saying them. "Can't take a chance. My dog is in the book. Paid a hundred dollars for him."

"I get the drift." Skeeter stepped back from the truck and Lady followed him and stood close to him. "Your dog's in the book and mine came from the swamp. Well, I aim to keep mine."

"That's what I told him," Jesse said. "Told him we'd be rightly proud to look after his, but that we aim to keep ours."

"Know how you feel," Cash said. "But I aim to take mine over to the Watson place and get Gates to look after him, and work him out every day. Your dog won't be running over that way, will she?"

Uncle Jesse started to speak and then held his tongue and deferred to the boy. After all, Lady was his dog and he should speak. Skeeter thought for a second to find the words he wanted and then he found them. "I'll keep my dog this side of the river. I won't let her run with your dog and learn him bad habits. But you keep yours on the other side of the river."

"I'll tell Gates." Cash stepped on the starter. "No hard feelings."

"No hard feelings," Skeeter said. "Just tell Gates I said keep your dog away from mine and I'll keep mine away from yours."

"Just tell Gates we both said that," Uncle Jesse added.

Cash put his truck into gear and told them good-bye and that he would be seeing them, and he drove away.

The old man and the boy watched the truck out of sight and the dust settling and then Uncle Jesse walked back toward the cabin and the woodpile. "Put the buttermilk inside," he said. "Then come on and we'll finish that wood."

"Did Mister Cash say anything about the wood?"

"He'll pick it up in a few days."

Skeeter caught up with Uncle Jesse and Lady ran ahead of them. "Is there enough wood there to square our bill?"

"Just about."

They got to the porch and the boy picked up the buckets and started in the front door and then he stopped and turned. "How much did Mister Cash offer if we'd look after his dog?"

"Not so much."

"How much, Uncle Jesse?"

"Three dollars a week and his som'n t'eat."

The amount surprised the boy and he turned the figure in his mind. Such a sum in a few months would mean
Uncle Jesse's false teeth and maybe down payment on
a .20 gauge shotgun. The boy opened the door and Lady
dashed in and leaped on his bed and curled up and he
himself stood there in the doorway and was dejected;
yes, downright miserable. "Heard a bull 'gator the other
day. Get him, come cool weather. Hide'll sell good." He
did not raise his eyes from the floor. "And there's bound
to be some bee gums that the bears didn't get. They'll
bring four, five dollars. And we can cut a heap of wood
between now and rainy weather. Do most of the cutting
myself, Uncle Jesse. We'll get them Roebuckers."

The old man sidled over into the shade and stared at
the woodpile and then he sighed and headed back to the
saw. "Don't fret yourself about it. Did I get them Roebuckers I'd eat so many roastin' ears I'd get down with
heartburn or som'n, mor'n likely."

CHAPTER ∽ ∽ ∽ ∽ ∽ SIX

Skeeter lost no time in beginning lady's lessons as a bird hunter and while Uncle Jesse worked at the saw the boy kept his dog in the swamp and in the brush and disciplined her for her work. First, she had to learn to come to him when he called her and to stay where he commanded.

And had he loved her one whit less and had his pride not been so full upon him, then his patience would have been worn out in the chore of teaching her to hunt only birds, for Lady was eager to hunt anything.

In the beginning, she was baffled by his command for her to heel and to walk always at his left and only a few steps behind him, or to sit motionless or stand patiently at his left heel when he told her to. He got the frayed old rope and tied a loop around her neck and made her follow him at the proper distance and at the proper gait. If she came too close, he pushed her back and if she straggled, he pulled her close; and all the time he kept saying to her, "Heel, Lady. Heel."

Over and over he did this while they walked through the swamp and across the piney ridge and into the broom straw and then back to the swamp. Once she tried to dash away and chase a rabbit and he pinched the rope around her neck, and although the pain was slight the humiliation was much, and her eyes filled and he pinched even harder. "Don't gimme that crying stuff," he told her. "Used to get by with Uncle Jesse doing that my-self."

She must have understood because it took her only a few hours to associate disobedience with disfavor, and she learned quickly that the boy would reward good work, but that he also could punish without pity.

The first lesson was learned so easily that it bothered Skeeter because her behavior convinced him that she had been disciplined before, that she had had another master. He had been in the woods all morning of the first day and by middle sun, the day half away, she was at his heel and never budging, always watching his eyes if he turned to her and her ears always forward to catch his words even when he spoke them softly, even when he whispered them.

Skeeter was hungry and knew that she must be hungry, too, and so he took the rope from her neck and commanded her to follow him and she did, and they both were very tired when they got back to the cabin. Uncle Jesse was sawing wood and the sawdust clung to his eyebrows and to his sweaty shirt. Any other man would have removed his shirt for such work, but never Jesse Jackson, for he was a swamper and his back must be clothed in public and his head covered. His shirt was his pride, as was his hat, and it mattered not how dirty and sweaty was his shirt or how slouchy his hat—they were his pride and must be worn. He scarcely glanced up when the boy and the dog walked across the yard, and Skeeter said, "I'm hungry. My stomach must think my throat's been cut."

"Then go get som'n t'eat. I done et."

"Anything left I can feed my dog?" He tossed the rope on the woodpile and stretched his tired muscles.

"Feed her tonight." Uncle Jesse shoved another piece of wood into the saw and the whine was so shrill that he had to shout above it to be heard.

"But she's hungry."

The old man turned from his work and spoke solemnly: "Never feed a grown dog but once't a day. Always at night. Dogs want to sleep after they done et."

"Sleep if she wants to. Ain't going out this evening."
Evening meant afternoon.

"Believe I would, if it was me." Uncle Jesse began
stacking the wood he had cut. "Believe I'd stay with it."

Skeeter moved to help him. "Sort of figured on stick-
ing around here and helping you out."

"You stay with your job and I'll stay with mine."
Uncle Jesse looked up at the sun and knew that the saw
would be in the shade in about an hour and that pleased
him. "You run the dog and I'll run the saw."

The boy told Lady to lie down and stay with Uncle
Jesse and she did, choosing for herself a nice cool spot
in the shade of the woodpile. "Stay right there," Skeeter
said. "Be back t'reckly."

He went into the cabin and Uncle Jesse watched him
through the door and then looked down at the dog. "You
learn fast," he said to her. "Got sense enough to get in
the shade and to stay put where he says."

She pricked up her ears and watched him and he, too,
knew that she had been disciplined before, that she had
had another master. He reached down and lifted a heavy
piece of wood and grunted as he did so, and Lady tilted
her head at him and chuckled. Uncle Jesse hurled his
burden from him and scowled down at her. "What's so
blamed funny? Me in the sun and you in the shade. Me
sawing and you resting."

127

He picked up the lightest piece of wood that was within reach and shoved it hard into the saw, muttering to himself and again Lady tilted her head and chuckled.

Skeeter came out of the cabin and buttermilk was on his upper lip and Uncle Jesse said to him, "Wipe your mouth."

He wiped it on his sleeve and then Uncle Jesse said, "Did you find enough t'eat?"

"Yes, sir. Them cold potatoes that Aunt Bonnie Dew sent us and some buttermilk." He sat down in the shade by Lady and scratched her back and behind her ears. "Reckon I better get on back to the woods."

"Reckon you should."

"Sort of tired, though."

"Me, too." Uncle Jesse slicked the sawdust from his sweaty hands and wished the sun would hurry behind the water oak that would throw shade across the saw. "Want yourself a bird dog, so stay with it."

"Ever' day?"

"Ever' day. From can 'til can't. From itch to ache. Only way to train a bird dog. Stay with it ever' day."

The boy lifted the rope and slung it over his shoulder and walked away and the dog followed him and they went back to the swamp and the lessons began all over again—"Heel, Lady. Heel."

By mid-afternoon Skeeter was so tired he sought a log

deep in the shade and sat down and drooped his head to
his chest and closed his eyes. Lady was tired, too, and
she curled at his feet and they both rested and then suddenly she tilted her nose and leaped to her feet and was
away, ripping toward the river despite his commands
that she return. He ran after her and then he heard the
chicken squawking and when he found his dog she was
eating a big fat Dominecker hen.

The boy was horrified. The chicken belonged to the
Watsons and had got across the river somehow and Lady
had smelled it from afar. The boy snatched the chicken
from her and beat her across the nose with it. He looked
around carefully to be sure nobody had seen the incident
and he got a stick and dug a hole in the muck and buried
the evidence deep and pulled a log over it. No one must
know that she had killed the chicken. A chicken-killing
dog, like an egg-sucking dog, could not live in the
swamp, for any man had the right to shoot a chicken-
killer or an egg-sucker.

The Watsons might never miss the chicken and even
if they did they would have no idea what had happened
to it. Nevertheless, the boy was scared. Having tasted
chicken blood, his dog would want more and Skeeter
didn't know what to do. He grabbed her by the scruff
of the neck and cuffed her hard. "Chicken-killer!" He
spat out the verdict and she cringed from him. "No

wonder Mister Cash didn't want you running with his dog."

Lady slunk away from him and lay down and put her paws over her face and her eyes filled.

"Chicken dog." He walked over and sat down by her. "Ain't you got any sense? Don't you know that a chicken dog and a suck-egg dog ain't no-count? Ain't you got a lick of sense?" He was so exasperated that he felt like crying and yet he yearned to pet her, but that wouldn't do at all. So he ordered her to follow him and they went deeper into the swamp and up toward the bayou and she stayed right at his heels until they were almost to the bayou and then she cut around in front of him and looked over her shoulder at him, and chuckled. And then, deliberately, she dashed away. He was so surprised that he stood there for a minute and didn't even call her. She ran toward the bayou and he got out his pocket knife and cut a heavy green switch and followed her.

She was eating the water rat when he found her. There was no need to whip her because now he realized that she was not afraid of blows and cuffs. She must be shamed and so he threw the switch away and unravelled more of the rope and tied the dead rat around her neck. She pawed at the thing as she had at the other one and tried to shake it loose and, failing this, she looked up at him as though begging him to free her of this hated burden.

"Got to wear it." He drew the noose tighter around her neck and the dead rat was against her throat. "Can't help if folks do see it and know you're a rat-runner."

It was a badge she must wear even if it did reveal her weakness, even if it did disgrace her master; and it did— for all who saw it would know that Skeeter and Uncle Jesse had a no-count rat dog; no hunter at all, but just a no-count rat dog that might even sink low enough to chase chickens and suck eggs.

It was time to go home because evening gloam was nigh and, yet, as weary as he was, the boy dreaded to go home. The first rat wasn't so bad. His dog didn't know any better then. But this one was different. She had done it a second time and that was a shame on her and a slur on him.

The sun was far down behind the swamp when Skeeter walked into the cabin and Lady slunk in behind him and stood trembling by the door. Uncle Jesse was fixing supper and he glanced down at her and saw the rat around her neck and looked away quickly, for a man does not stare at shame.

Skeeter said nothing and Uncle Jesse said nothing, and Lady crawled over to the old man and rubbed against his leg, begging him to help her and to take off the symbol and throw it away. He pushed her from him, shoving her aside with his foot and he, too, seemingly was without pity or even sympathy.

She slunk away from both of them and went to Skeeter's bed and leaped up on it and the boy went over and grabbed her by the scruff of her neck and jerked her off. "No rat dog sleeps in my bed," he said bitterly.

So she crawled under the bed and kept pawing at the thing, but it would not come off and she lay there sobbing her misery and mortification; and was utterly alone because the old man and the boy sat down at the table and ate their supper and did not speak her name or even glance her way.

Skeeter piled all the scraps into a pan and put it by the edge of the bed. She would not show her face, though, even for food and the boy turned his back to her without so much as a word and went to the front porch and got the water bucket and helped Uncle Jesse wash the dishes.

The old man put the lamp in the middle of the table and he and the boy sat down and looked at each other and Skeeter said, "Maybe she was hungry. Maybe that's how come she did like she did."

"Rat dog. Ain't no two ways about it, you got a rat dog on your hands."

"Maybe she'll learn better."

132

"Hard to break a rat dog." He spoke it as though he hated to say it. "She mout even be a chicken dog or a suck egger."

Skeeter didn't dare tell him about the chicken. "Aim to leave the rat on and let her get a bait of it."

"How long?" Uncle Jesse lit his pipe and rubbed his shoulder muscles that ached from the strain of the day.

"All night. Maybe tomorrow night. What you think?"

"That'll be long enough. A dead rat ain't rightly nice around the house."

"She'll be broke by then."

"Hope so. A rat dog ain't worth feeding. Never saw a rat dog make a bird dog." His pipe was clogged up and he got a broom straw and cleaned it. "Hope she don't go after chickens or eggs. Somebody'd shoot her, sure as the Lord made little apples."

"Like I told you, maybe she was just hungry. Any dog will go after a rat if he's hungry."

"Do she be hungry, how come she don't eat?"

There was no answer to that and so they just sat there in the flickering lamplight and each with his own thoughts and neither saying a word; and Lady cowering under the bed and her food untouched.

The moths and other insects were swarming around the lamp and dying and the old man reached out his long bony hand and brushed the dead ones from the table.

"Need a little stove wood," he said. "Didn't bring in none today. Too busy cutting."

Skeeter never before had brought in stove wood at night and he looked over at the wood box and there was plenty of wood there for breakfast. However, he did not argue or even say a word, but got the lantern and lit it and went out into the night.

Uncle Jesse waited until he heard him at the wood-pile and then he got the can of bacon drippings from the back of the stove and went over to the boy's bed. He dared not move the lamp for fear Skeeter would see him. He got on his hands and knees and reached under the bed and patted Lady and then he poured the bacon drippings on her food. "Come on and eat it," he said to her and spoke very softly.

She thumped her tail against the floor and crawled from under the bed and licked his face and then pawed at the rat, entreating him to remove it.

"I ain't in this." He stroked her back and felt her trembling under his touch. This here is between you and the boy. Talk to him come daybust, though. Mout'n take it off then and not wait 'til sundown. See what I can do. Now eat."

She did as he asked and ate the food as though she were doing him a favor and he kept talking to her: "You had oughta stick by the boy and do like he says. He went out on a limb for you and you hadn't oughta cut it off. He stood up to ol' Cash for you and wouldn't let him low-rate you. You got to stick by the boy; me and you, both." He looked closely at her in the soft light from the lamp across the room and saw the tiny pin feathers still clinging to the corners of her mouth. Chicken feathers. He was as horrified as Skeeter had been and he grabbed her ear and held her tight and carefully removed the pin feathers. Maybe Skeeter didn't know and he would never tell him. Or maybe he did know and was keeping it to himself. Either way, it was a thing he would not take up with the boy. If Skeeter knew that his dog was a chicken killer as well as a rat dog, then it was his hurt and, therefore, a sorrow to be shared only upon invitation. If he didn't know, then he would never know from the old man.

So Uncle Jesse destroyed the evidence and, hearing Skeeter returning, he hastened to put the can of bacon drippings back on the stove and went to his chair at the table and picked up his pipe. Lady still was eating and the rat got in her way and she kept pawing it aside, but it would not be gone and clung to her like a stain; this repulsive symbol of her weakness.

Skeeter dropped the wood into the box and saw that Lady was out from under the bed and eating, and saw the grease on the food and knew what had happened.

He looked a long time at Uncle Jesse and the old man felt guilty. "The bacon dripping can was too full," he explained. "So I gave her a little bit. Grease will make her hide slick. Good for the natures, too."

"Is that the way to train a dog? Me trying to learn her to do right and you up and give her bacon grease. Is that right?"

"No, I reckon not." The old man felt sheepish and would not look at the boy. "Didn't mean to butt in. Just sort of felt sorry for her. Hungry and hiding under the bed and a dead rat around her neck."

"I'm glad you did it. It's all right as long as I didn't do it. She's got to know that I won't stand for no messing around."

He got some hickory nuts and cracked some for the old man and mashed them and the old man ate them and then the night things came out, calling and crying, and the whip-poor-wills calling from the ridge and the swamp squirming in its sleep.

"Like me to read to you?" the boy asked. "Know you're tired and I'll read 'til you get sleepy, if you want me to."

"I'd like a little reading. Don't know nothing I'd like more than a little reading. 'Cept maybe some roast'n ears or som'n like that."

The boy went over to a stack of old magazines that

136

Cash Evans had brought out weeks before and he fingered through them, the picture magazines and sports magazines and many other kinds. "Do you want I should read about the Space Man?" He had picked up a comic book. "You know—about that fellow who can turn hisself into a big solid gold bird. Big'n a buzzard and fly over mountains and things like that. Want me to read about him? The Space Man?"

"Never mind. Can't nothing turn itself into som'n like that."

"Snollygosters do. Into frogs. Tadpoles and snollygosters turn into frogs."

"That's different. So let's have us one about cowboys. You know me. Just naturally cotton to cowboys."

Skeeter found a western story magazine that was dirty and dog-eared and splotched with grease where it had laid on the counter of Cash Evans' store. He thumbed through it to a likely-looking story and went back to the table and pulled the lamp close to the edge of the table and began reading, and he thanked the Lord that most of the words were easy.

Uncle Jesse slouched in his chair and puffed his pipe and took in the beauty of the words he did not understand, the words about marvels that only his fancy could picture; the prairies so different from the swamp and so far away. The hard dry gulches, the brave men, the

137

brave land—the never-felt land of his own boyhood dreams.

Out there the winds sang high and free. Thus the words said. Here in his world the winds hummed and sobbed, crying for something that had no answer—like something never seen but only felt and this something touching the strings to the heart of an unlettered old man who could not speak the things he felt and who felt them all the more because he could not speak them: the aching hurt of being old and the happy sorrow of watching a boy grow up and knowing that he, too, must wear a symbol around his neck, that he, like all men, must carry some foul thing forever, some weakness— and also knowing that some day the swamp winds, the home sounds so long remembered, would feel for the strings to the boy's heart and bring forth only the echo of the melody of what used to be—the beauty of the sprouting years, the hope of longing, then the misery of loving something that must grow old; all this the mystery that the old man felt and could not say, this miracle of man's life on God's earth.

The boy stumbled on a word and Uncle Jesse opened his eyes and then the boy struggled through the word and the old man nodded approval and closed his eyes again, and his mind unshackled itself from its gloom and soared free to the big mountains that had snow on them, to the land where grass was belly deep; and he believed it all, every sound of it.

Lady heard the words, too; the droning of the boy's voice and she licked the last bits of food from the pan and cocked her head from side to side, watching them. She was lonesome over in the shadows by the bed and the lamp was bright and warm, and the boy's voice droning. She crawled toward them, dragging the rat, and her ears were tilted to catch Skeeter's summons if he spoke it, if he invited her to join them.

The boy paid her no mind; none.

She stood up and shook herself and chuckled, and still he ignored her, just reading the words, and so she walked over and rubbed against the leg of his chair and then against his own leg and still he read on and had no word for her, and so she curled at his feet and put her head on her paws and watched him.

He finished the story. It took him a long time to finish it and Uncle Jesse was almost asleep. "That was a good'n." Skeeter closed the magazine and studied the picture on the front, the blob of grease on the face of the beautiful girl and the streak of grime on the cowboy.

"Crackerjack." Uncle Jesse opened his eyes and his mind came back from the high prairies that he had never seen, from the clean treeless land, back to the swamp and the crawling night. "Sure wish I'd been a cowboy."

"Rather be a railroad engineer myself."

"Had a chance to go to Texas once't. That's where they got cowboys. In Texas."

"Then I could run a train all the way to Mobile and I wouldn't stop at Mobile but keep right on plum' to Atlanta and places like that, just balling the jack, high-tailing it to who laid a chunk, just go and go, lickety-split."

"Seen a cowboy once't. Ol' Buffalo Bill. Seen him in a sideshow." Uncle Jesse knocked the ashes from his pipe onto the table and then brushed them into his hand and threw them onto the wood box. "Wonder how come ol' Cash didn't name that dog of his'n Buffalo Bill. Now there's a good name. But Millard Fillmore—" He shook his head at the puzzle of it all. "Just because nothing else ain't ever been named such as that cep'n a President of the United States. Ain't no figuring Cash Evans. Just ain't no figuring the man."

Skeeter felt his dog's cold nose against his bare feet and she was licking his feet and he hurt to reach down and pat her, and yet he wouldn't, but got up and walked away from her and took the magazine back to the pile. "I'm sleepy."

"Rightly tuckered myself." Uncle Jesse put the lamp

close to his bed so he could blow it out without any effort much.

Skeeter went to his own bed and Lady stayed by the table. Her head was on her paws and she just kept watching the boy, wishing that he would call her, or say something to her.

Then the old man and the boy were in their beds and the lamp was out and she was alone in the darkness. The moon was wasting and the door was open and the swamp was wide and big, and all the night things calling and crying. The cabin was very small with so little within except the old man and the boy, but there she stayed, watching the moon and the outside and then she walked over to the boy's bed and crawled under it.

Skeeter reached over and tapped the floor and she came out and he untied the rat and threw it out of the window and for a minute or so she stood by his bed and licked his hand and his face, and then she leaped in the bed and snuggled down beside him.

CHAPTER ～ ～ ～ SEVEN

CASH EVANS CAME BACK OUT TO THE CABIN ON THE
same day that Skeeter gave his dog her first lesson in
casting and the boy was so pleased with himself, and
with Lady, that he ran all the way home to report her
progress to Uncle Jesse.

The old man and Cash were sitting in the shade fanning themselves with their hats and when Skeeter saw
them he slowed to a walk because he didn't want
Mister Cash to know that he was excited. The boy's
dog was beside him and together they moseyed over to
the shade and Skeeter greeted the visitor politely but
with reserve, for he still was rankling with the knowledge that the storekeeper had segregated his Millard
Fillmore from Lady.

142

Cash felt called upon to explain his presence and so he said, "Came out to get my wood."

"All cut," Uncle Jesse said. "Pretty a'wood as I ever seen."

"That's a fact." The storekeeper stared down at the dog as though he might say something either to her or about her, but he didn't. "Seen myself a heap of wood." He was keeping the conversation away from the dog. "But never seen no wood no prettier than this here wood."

His tone was kind and Uncle Jesse's eyes were prideful and the combination told their story: the two old cronies were over their pout and everything was all right again. This gave Skeeter a feeling of well-being and security and for a reason that neither he nor Uncle Jesse had discussed, for it was so delicate.

Cash Evans was the only merchant thereabouts who ever had extended credit to Uncle Jesse, and supplies were running low and they had no money; and Skeeter had wondered what they would do as long as Uncle Jesse and Mister Cash had their habits on and were pouting.

There was another store about half a mile down the road from Mister Cash's, but it was run by a Negro and if Uncle Jesse asked for credit there and was refused, then that would be an humiliation comparable to general knowledge that the old man couldn't write; being refused credit by a Negro. But now, apparently, everything was all right again and that little gnawing hurt, really a fear, that had been inside Skeeter for several days was gone. So he spoke out confidently: "No doubt about it. Mighty fine wood. Uncle Jesse been cutting up a storm."

The old man basked in the praise and read the boy's mind and put his mind at ease by saying, "Ol' Cash says this wood will settle that little ol' frazzling account he been carrying for us. Squares us up. Ain't that so, Cash? Ain't that what you said?"

"Not for the saw. Squares for the supplies, but not for the saw."

"Saw don't count," Uncle Jesse said. "Long as we're squared for our som'n t'eat—that's all that counts."

"I'll help you load the wood." Skeeter was so happy that he even was ready to forgive Mister Cash for his insulting treatment of Lady. "I'll back your truck back in here, if you want me to."

"Better let ol' Cash do his own backing," Uncle Jesse said. "You might strip a gear or bust something—"

"Let him back it in," Cash said. "He can drive a truck good as me. Go ahead and back it in, Skeeter. Just step on the starter hard and shove her in gear and whip her back in here. You can do it."

Skeeter and Lady ran out to the truck and jumped into the cab and the boy felt like a man as he worked the truck by the side of the cabin and to the woodpile. He sprang out of the cab, and Lady too, and he began pitching wood into the truck.

"Mighty fine backing," Cash said. "Never saw nobody back back any better than that. How 'bout you, Jesse?"

"Pretty a'backing as I ever seen and I've seen myself some mighty fine backing, around lumber camps and on public works and things like that."

"You never worked at a lumber camp in your life." Cash sauntered away from Uncle Jesse. "Nor on public works, neither. You wouldn't even work on the W. P. and A." He pitched some wood into the truck, but was not working as hard as Skeeter who was working very hard.

Uncle Jesse picked up one stick of wood, the smallest one handy, and lobbed it into the truck. With Cash and the boy working so hard, there was no need for him to be so foolish and, besides, he had cut the wood. "Didn't say nothing about where I worked. Just said I'd seen some mighty fine backing."

"Seen me some fine backing, too." Cash took off his hat and mopped his brow and leaned against the truck. "Once't I put in a few licks a'ship-building down at

Mobile and them truck drivers down there were the prettiest backers I ever seen."

Uncle Jesse stepped back into the shade. "Now you're talking about backers what are backers."

Skeeter was the only one working and he straightened up and looked at them and at the woodpile, and Cash walked over to the shade and joined Jesse and spoke up real loud, "Never saw nobody load wood like that boy. Stout, ain't he?"

"Stout as a billy goat," Uncle Jesse said. "Wood-loading to who laid a chunk."

"Stout as a mule," Cash said. "Top hand backer and top hand loader, that's what I say."

The praise strengthened Skeeter and he worked even harder than before and soon was running sweat, but that didn't make any difference because Uncle Jesse and Mister Cash were friends again and the account was settled and they could get more stuff on credit and, besides, they had bragged on him.

There was a big hole in the woodpile and the truck was settling heavy when Uncle Jesse said, "Need me a drink of water."

"Me, too," Cash said.

"Want I should bring you a drink?" Uncle Jesse spoke to Skeeter.

"If it ain't too much trouble, I'd be obliged for a

drink of water." He kept on pitching wood.

The two men went into the cabin and the boy re-doubled his efforts, determined to have the truck loaded when they got back and thereby earn more praise. Even Lady deserted him and walked out of the sun and curled up in the cool shade of the water oak.

It took Uncle Jesse and Cash a long time to get a drink of water and the truck was loaded before they got back and Skeeter was sitting in the cab making believe he was driving the truck; his head out the cab window and his hands gripping the wheel as his fancy sped him over the play-like roads that all boys travel.

Cash had the water bucket with him and filled the dipper himself and handed it to the boy. "Didn't aim for you to finish so quick."

"Me, neither," Uncle Jesse said. "Figured on loading myself after I rested a little bit."

"Never saw a better load, though." Cash put the bucket by the side of the truck and Skeeter got out of the cab.

He went over and sat down on the cabin steps and opened his shirt and let in the breeze and Lady came over and licked his face and then went over to the water bucket and lapped up water.

Cash stooped to move the bucket away and then

thought better of it. "Is it all right for her to drink out of your bucket?"

"It's all right," Skeeter said. "Me and Uncle Jesse don't care. And you done had your water, so you won't be drinking after her."

"Me and the boy don't care if she drinks out'n the bucket," Uncle Jesse said. "She's the cleanest dog I ever seen, and the smartest. And I've seen me some smart dogs. She's a hunting fool."

"Whatcha mean—hunting?" Cash looked at Lady as she lapped up the water. "You standing there telling me that this is a hunting dog?"

"I'm standing here telling you," Uncle Jesse said. "She pints anything." He was laying it on thick, much too thick.

Skeeter was disturbed because Uncle Jesse was bragging too much and he was afraid that Mister Cash might call Uncle Jesse's hand and then Uncle Jesse would be humiliated. So he waited until the old man paused in his bragging and put in, "She's doing rightly good so far. Just this morning I waved her out and she cast—"

"Whatcha mean—cast?" Cash was skeptical.

Skeeter was on sure ground now and was confident. "Like I said, she cast this morning—"

"I'm from Missouri," Cash said. "You've got to show me—"

148

"The boy's tired," Uncle Jesse broke in quickly. He was afraid that Skeeter had been doing some big-talking and he aimed to give the boy an out if he needed an out.

"I ain't tired," Skeeter said. "Come on, I'll show you some casting." He got up from the steps and called to his dog and she bounded to him.

"She minds good," Cash said.

"You ain't seen nothing." Uncle Jesse glanced up at the sun and knew they had time for a turn in the woods. "Come on, me and the boy'll show you a dog."

Skeeter walked ahead of them and out of the yard and Lady trotted closely beside him and they went over the ridge and to a field of broomstraw. A breeze was rustling the sedge and the boy's long yellow hair, and the sun was slanting hot through the pine trees that rimmed the field and then Skeeter spoke a command to his dog and her ears came up and she looked at him and then away, turning her head slowly and raising her nose into the breeze.

"Sharp, ain't she?" Uncle Jesse spoke his praise very softly.

"Hunting proud," Cash said and by this he meant that she was sensitive and by no means arrogant or haughty.

Skeeter held out his hand and stroked her head and

her ears and knelt beside her and stroked her chest and whispered to her and she was trembling, and then he stood and called out, "Hup!" He waved his hand toward the field. "Hup, Lady. Birds!"

She lowered her nose to the ground and was away and slipped into the broomstraw and raised her nose high into the wind and chuckled, and then began racing across the field, covering it from side to side.

Skeeter glanced back at Uncle Jesse and smiled and the old man grinned and nudged Cash, and the store-keeper grinned, too, and then laughed. "Be John Brown! Look at that. Casting, sure as I'm standing here." He was as pleased as Skeeter and almost as pleased as Uncle Jesse.

"Whipping that field, ain't she?" Uncle Jesse rammed his hands in his pockets and r'ared back and watched her. "Covering that field like a fall of dew."

Quickly, Lady was out of sight in the broomstraw, working deep in it, and then she appeared on a rise to the east, tossed her head high for any scent that was on the breeze, and raced away again, ripping through the sedge and circling.

Skeeter said nothing. It was his privilege to brag, but he didn't. It was his right to big-talk about his dog and yet he denied himself the right and did not gloat but turned to Mister Cash and, in deep reserve, spoke most mannerably: "Aim to follow her?"

"Hunting proud," Cash said over and over and shook his head as though he scarcely could believe what he was seeing. "Beats all. Casting like a bird dog. Hound from pup to papa, but casting like a bird dog."

"Aim to follow her?" Skeeter repeated. "She's working fast and we'll lose her if we don't move on."

Cash started off first and they walked rapidly across the field, heading toward the bayou and the swamp beyond, and Lady flashed before them and was running easy through the sedge, never bounding, but running easy and covering the ground close and catching the breeze and the scents it bore.

"Never saw nothing prettier." Uncle Jesse had awe in his voice and bursting pride. "Like the boy said all along, she's a hunter."

"Ain't arguing so far," Cash said. "Acts like a bird dog, but is she hunting birds?"

"Ain't saying." Skeeter felt called upon to protect his dog and himself. "Ain't tried to learn her to get birds. Not yet. Whatcha expect so soon?"

Lady was out of sight in a thick growth and the two men and the boy walked to a knoll and stood there looking around and waiting for her to reappear. The bayou drifted by the edge of the field and Cash was the first to see Gates Watson standing by the bayou and looking their way, and he said, "Yonder's Gates. Standing there like a stump."

"His skiff's tied to that ol' dead gum," Uncle Jesse said. "He come over in his skiff. Wonder what he's up to?"

And then they saw the chickens, five or six big Domineckers scratching along the bank of the bayou and Gates shooing them toward his boat. The chickens were clucking and fussing and Gates was waving his arms and then he looked over at the two men and the boy again, and called a greeting.

It was then that Lady dashed out of the undergrowth and wheeled toward the bayou and froze to a point. Her curved tail poked up over her back and she spraddled her front legs and sort of squatted and her nose was toward the bayou and the chickens there.

Gates glanced at his chickens and up at the dog and stepped back into the shadows. Uncle Jesse grunted and looked at Skeeter and the boy's lips started quivering and he struggled within himself to hold back his tears and his mortification.

"Chicken dog," Cash Evans said contemptuously. "She's pointing them chickens."

There was nothing for Skeeter to say. There were the chickens and there was his dog on a frozen point, her nose low toward the ground and her tail rigid. He wanted to cry out that he hadn't had a chance to teach her about birds, but only to obey his commands and to cast; that the rest would come later, that they expected too much from a waif dog. But he said nothing, only hurting deeply within himself.

It was Uncle Jesse who spoke for her because the aged have more faith than the young and this is a truth that man alone really knows about himself; that the old have faith and the young only hopes. So Uncle Jesse said, "She's got birds."

Cash laughed at him. "You're crazy. She's got chickens."

"She's got birds." It almost was a whisper as though he were saying it to himself and to any miracle power that would heed the yearning of toothless old age. "I'm standing here and saying she's got birds." He said it so calmly that Skeeter turned and looked at him and saw there the serenity and confidence of a man proclaiming a miracle because a miracle was meet and right.

"It's chickens, Uncle Jesse." The boy strained the words through the anguish of his hurt. "Ain't no use of saying it ain't. My dog's pointing chickens."

"I'm standing here saying she's got birds. Go to your dog, boy. Flush them birds and get her off that point. She'll stand there till judgment day. She'll hold right there until you let her break. She's telling you she's got birds and you got to believe her."

Lady turned her head slightly and looked back, but at the old man and not at the boy at all and then Skeeter, only to please the old man, stepped to his dog's side and into the sedge before her; and then a whirr and a flurry of wings and the quail were up and away.

Cash Evans forgot that the boy was nigh and took the name of his God, shouting his amazement. "Great God A'mighty! She had birds! Casted and pinted and held them." He began jumping up and down in his excitement and his little pot-belly bounced and he jerked off his hat and threw it to the ground and jumped up and down some more. "Seen it myself. Me standing right here and I seen it."

"Told you she had birds." Uncle Jesse's voice still was calm.

Skeeter just stood there, peering at his dog and at where the covey of quail had been, the broomstraw waving in the breeze and his dog at his feet and looking up at him. Then he knelt by her and the tears came and he put his arms around her neck and rubbed his cheek against her face. "My little ol' dog. My little ol' dog."

Uncle Jesse stood apart and in the dignity of a prophet, but Cash went to the boy and he, too, knelt by the dog and stroked her and muttered his praises of her triumph. "A hunter born," he said. "And a hunter bred."

"Maybe." The boy's pride was far removed from the modesty of his word.

"Is she gun shy?" Cash felt the muscles of her front legs and the depth of her chest. "Can you shoot over her?"

Skeeter sniffed and brushed his sleeve across his nose and stood up, struggling for the dignity that came so naturally to Uncle Jesse. "Ain't had a chance to shoot over her yet. Can't shoot quail until a cool spell hits and that'll be two, almost three months."

"She's got a hard mouth." Cash ran his hand under her lower jaw. "She'll fetch rough and tear birds."

"She'll learn." It was a boast and Skeeter did not mean for it to be, but now he felt that Lady could do anything.

"You know how to break her of hard-mouthing." The storekeeper gave the dog one more pat and stood up and watched her walk over to Skeeter and stand at his side.

"Wire stick?" Skeeter asked and then looked away from Mister Cash and toward Uncle Jesse who was standing so near and yet who seemed so far apart, for such was his gravity and silence.

"Wire stick is best," Cash said. "Just wrap some

wire around a stick and make her tote it and fetch it. She won't bite down. That'll break her of hard mouth. Some folks use bob-wire."

"I'll use baling wire. Bob-wire will stick her. Ain't that what you say, Uncle Jesse?"

"Knew she had birds." The old man looked hard at the dog, then off toward the swamp and the blue haze over the river and the sun dancing through the trees. "Said right out loud that she had birds, and she had 'em."

Gates Watson walked up from the bayou and added his praise. "Thought at first she was pointing those chickens and then I heard Mr. Jesse say that she had birds. It sure was a sight."

"What them chickens doing down there?" Cash demanded. "Them your Domineckers, Gates?"

"They're mine. Found a tree leaning over the river and got on this side. You know how chickens are. I was trying to round them up."

"How many got across?" Skeeter's voice rose in his anxiety.

"Seven."

"Did you find them all?" The boy was almost afraid to ask.

"Found them all," Gates said without a flicker of hesitation.

"Yes, sir. Knew she had birds and spoke right out, and she had 'em." Uncle Jesse was above the discourse and in the reverie of the wonder.

"How my dog doing?" Cash asked. "How ol' Mill getting along?"

"All right," Gates said. "Work him every day. Course, there are more birds on this side of the river than on our side."

"There's enough over there to keep my dog working." Cash stooped and picked up his hat and beat it against his leg to shake off the dust and then put it on and started away.

Gates smiled at Skeeter and bragged on his dog again and said so long to Mr. Jesse. "Sure am glad I found my chickens. Lost seven and found seven. Afraid a 'gator or some varmint might have got one, but found them all."

"I'm glad, too," Skeeter said. "Be seeing you, Gates. Drop by if you're over our way."

Uncle Jesse turned and followed Cash, and Gates went his way and Skeeter spoke to Lady and the two men and the boy and the dog retraced their steps home. Uncle Jesse went straight to the shade of the water oak and sat down there on the soft earth and took off his hat and leaned his head against the tree, and Lady went to him and he pulled her close and rubbed her.

Mister Cash let Skeeter drive the truck out of the road and when he came back the storekeeper said, "Get your tablet and pencil. You folks got to have supplies."

The mention of supplies brought Uncle Jesse back to earth. "Running a mite low," he said.

Skeeter hurried for paper and pencil and rested the tablet on his knee and waited for Uncle Jesse to speak, but it was the storekeeper who spoke: "Put down baking powder first. And get it right."

He did.

"Now put down meat. You'll need some good middlin' meat and some beef."

Uncle Jesse's face lit up and he put on his hat and pulled the brim low over his eyes.

Skeeter wrote as Mister Cash directed and never before had he written such a list: a whole page of good things and down to three cans of peaches, nice, soft peaches that Uncle Jesse could chew.

The storekeeper checked the list and complimented the boy. Then he said to Uncle Jesse, "Come on. I'll drive you in town and fill this list and drive you back."

Uncle Jesse got slowly to his feet, as though he were doing the storekeeper a favor, and they walked out to the truck and Skeeter went with them and called good-bye to Mister Cash. "Glad you dropped by," he said. "Drop by any time."

"If baling wire don't work, then use bob-wire. You can't let her hard-mouth on you." Cash put his truck into gear and they were off, Uncle Jesse sitting very straight in the cab and his hat no longer low over his eyes, but on the back of his head in jaunty elation.

Skeeter took in a load of stove wood and filled the box to the top. He even went to the spring for a fresh bucket of water although the bucket was not empty. He lit a fire in the stove and started supper and put on a porringer for corn meal mush. Uncle Jesse liked corn meal mush and the boy aimed for him to have a bait of it. He used the last bit of middlin' meat and boiled it for Lady and mixed it with cold corn bread. There would be more middlin' meat, so it didn't matter if he used it all. He even gave her a can of pork and beans and felt good in this rare experience of extravagance.

It was the pink of evening and dry weather locusts were rasping in the water oak and the fireflies were out when Uncle Jesse got home and the load he fetched was so big that it took the two of them to bring all the good things into the cabin. They arranged them on the shelf and put the canned peaches to the front and they stepped back and looked at them and Uncle Jesse said, "Just look at 'em. Look at all that good stuff."

"Supper is almost ready," the boy said. "I cooked you some mush."

"Fed the dog?"

"Yes, sir. Gave her the last of that old middlin' meat and a can of pork and beans."

"Give her some more. Cut off a hunk of that beef and give her. And me and you gonna have us a can of peaches." He sat at the table and Skeeter brought his food and the old man spooned the mush into his mouth and some of it trickled to his chin and he wiped it away on his sleeve. "This here has been a day."

"How was everything at the store?"

"You oughta seen me. Me and ol' Cash rode up and he went in and took out that list and read it out loud and then sort of hollered: 'Jesse Jackson puts down the best list I ever seen and this here is one of the best orders I ever filled, fit'n for a big house or a revival meeting; fit'n for a big Delta planter at picking time.' That's what he said."

"Aw, Uncle Jesse, sure enough is that what he said?"

"That's what he said. And a heap of folks heard him and I reckon now folks'll know who's got credit around here and who puts down the best list."

He finished his mush and reached for the peaches and gave one of the slices to Lady and then supper was over and the boy said, "Want me to read?"

"Like a little reading."

"Cowboys?"

"I ain't choosey. Maybe you can find a good'un about som'n else."

The boy found one about ships and treasure and the old man closed his eyes and puffed his pipe while the boy read it through and then Uncle Jesse said, "Know'd she had birds."

He hadn't heard the story at all.

CHAPTER ∽ ∽ ∽ EIGHT

Dog days came in steaming heat and swooshing rains and the locusts shed their skins and the moon was red, and there was a ring around it. The bull alligators bellowed every night and the catfish swam far up the bayous and the crawfish dug deep.

Uncle Jesse spent most of his time in the swamp cutting cypress knees and traded them to Cash Evans who steamed them and peeled them and trucked them to Mobile where tourists paid fancy prices for the twisted and gnarled novelties.

Ordinarily Skeeter would have worked alongside Uncle Jesse in the muck and water around the cypress knees, but now he gave his days to his dog and went

162

with her every day to the fields, come rain and high water.

He wrapped wire around a stick and taught her to fetch and when she bit hard she learned better, and then he got bird feathers and tied them to a pine cone and she learned to retrieve it without crushing the feathers. The hard mouth became a soft mouth and that was good.

Every night he reported the day's progress to Uncle Jesse and sometimes his enthusiasm led into exaggeration and the old man never questioned the tales, only nodded solemnly and shared the boy's moods of triumph and fancy.

"Beats all get-out," Skeeter said one night when the wind swished up from the Gulf and fanned the supper lamp bright and then flickered it low. "Getting to where I don't even have to speak to her; just look at her and she knows what to do."

"Is that a fact?" The old man had been cutting cypress all day and an aching weariness was upon him and he was too tired to talk.

"It's a fact. Sitting here telling you." The boy stuffed food into his mouth and tried to talk at the same time and Uncle Jesse frowned and the boy was silent until he had swallowed the food. "Hid my pine cone and told her to go get it and she looked at me and laughed out loud like something was funny—something that I didn't know nothing about, and that she wished she could tell me but she couldn't and so she just laughed out loud; like something was funny."

"You don't say." A gusty rain blew up quick and the wind moaned under the cabin and around the eaves and seeped inside, and the lamp light bent low and sprang up bright and sent prancing shadows around the walls.

"I'm saying. So she lit out and found that pine cone and brought it to me and laughed again. She laughs all the time now and I ain't seen her fill up and go teary in quite a spell. Just laughs like she's doing what she likes—running and hunting and having herself a time."

"Well, now, I do declare."

"Aim to shoot over her pretty soon. Soon as it chills up and birds are fit'n, then I aim to shoot over her and break her to the gun and then shoot me and you a mess of partridge."

Uncle Jesse got up and looked around for a crocus sack and found one behind the stove and wedged it under the back door where the rain was blowing in. Then he lifted the coffeepot and took it back to the table and refilled his cup and the boy reached for a cup and pushed it toward the old man. Uncle Jesse filled it half full and the boy looked at him with a question in his eyes and Uncle Jesse nodded and reluctantly the boy picked up the can of milk and weakened his coffee and drank it.

And thus it was and one day was like the next and then the red moon wasted and the circle went away and autumn crept down from the north and brought the dry winds that blew the clouds high; and the ducks began flying and all night they passed high against the moon. The swamp shook some of her leaves from her back and dressed down for winter, stripping the red from the dogwood and the yellows from the hickorys.

But the pines and live oaks got greener, for winter was not a time of vivid change in the swamp, only a few trees coloring bright and then they were naked and stark and waved their hard, bare arms toward the river that was bellyful and swelling yellow.

The acorns were down and the mast was falling when Cash Evans came out that day, and Millard Fillmore was with him. Skeeter saw the storekeeper drive up and called Uncle Jesse and Lady and the three of them went out to the truck and then the boy saw Mister Cash's dog and wondered just what Mister Cash had on his mind and what he was up to.

Lady saw the big bird dog, too, and braced herself and cocked her head and watched him. Skeeter stood by her side and Mister Cash called out, "Brought ol' Mill along."

"So you did," Uncle Jesse said. "Brought ol' Mill along, huh?"

"He won't bother your dog." Mister Cash spoke to the boy. "Needn't fret yourself. Ol' Mill won't jump your dog."

Skeeter was too polite to remind the storekeeper that Lady had been able to take care of herself against the hog dogs and Gabe, and Uncle Jesse said nothing about it either, but glanced over at Skeeter and grinned. Cash read the grin and made a fussy thing of getting out of his truck. His dog jumped out and stood beside him and his head was high as he watched Lady and his tail fanned a friendly greeting. But Lady's tail was rigid and her hackle bristled her warning that she was on her own territory and that the visitor was an intruder.

Skeeter stooped and stroked her and Mister Cash said, "Sure is a pretty day."

"Sure is," said Uncle Jesse and looked from Lady to Millard Fillmore and hoped there would be no trouble.

"Rightly nice," Skeeter said. And again he wondered what the storekeeper was up to and why he should bring his dog to this side of the river after all the to-do about keeping the dogs separated.

"Never saw none prettier." Cash snapped a leash on his dog. "Bobwhites whistling in the broomstraw and a nice nip in the air. Just thought I'd come out to see you and bring my dog along."

"Always welcome," Uncle Jesse said. "Come on in and sit awhile and I'll make some coffee."

"Rightly obliged, Jesse. Just thought I'd bring my dog out here and let him run these ridges. Mess of quail this side of the river."

"Lots of partridge and lots of ridges." Uncle Jesse glanced at Skeeter, thus telling him that it was polite for him to say something.

"Plenty of quail for all," the boy said quickly. "Me and my dog aim to work that broomstraw over yonder across that north ridge. Plenty birds around the south ridge if you and your dog want to work over there."

Mister Cash reached back in the truck and got his jacket and slipped it on over his flannel shirt. "Don't see why they can't run together, mine and yours."

It was Uncle Jesse's place to speak, for Skeeter was yet a boy and important decisions must come from the old man and so the old man said, "You had your say a while back, Cash. Now what you saying?"

The storekeeper did not hesitate. "Saying I was wrong, that's what I'm saying. Me keeping mine on the other side. Even Gates said I was wrong."

Now it was proper for Skeeter to speak up and he was as quick with forgiveness as he was with resentment. "Be rightly proud to have your dog work along-side mine."

Thus the issue was closed and because it was closed it was forgotten, for such was the way of swamp folks. Cash freed his dog from the leash and the big setter dashed over to Lady to introduce himself, only to be rebuffed. The bristles of her hackle lay smooth, but she tossed her head and turned away from him and was dis-dainful of his presence. "Look at her," Cash said. "Big-chairing him. Sitting in the big rocker and looking down at him."

"Like he done her first time you brought him out here," Uncle Jesse said. "Now she's putting him below the salt."

Skeeter spoke to Lady to correct her manners, but he didn't speak too firmly because, truthfully, he was a bit pleased by Lady's behavior. "Don't big-chair him," he said to her. "He wants to be your friend."

But Lady walked proudly away from all of them and Millard Fillmore was baffled and sprawled on the ground and looked at her and then rolled over to impress her. Still she ignored him and he crawled toward her, wag-ging his tail in a futile bid for her attention.

"Keeping him outside the ribbon," Cash said. "But she'll get over it. Do her good to run with ol' Mill."

"Whatcha mean—good?" The question was sharper than Skeeter had intended for it to be.

"Mean she can learn from ol' Mill, him being such a good bird dog. She'll pick up tricks. That's one reason I brought him over—to help you out."

"Now, that was rightly nice." Uncle Jesse walked over to the shelter of the cabin and out of the nipping wind.

Skeeter and Mister Cash went over and joined him, and Lady disappeared behind the cabin and Millard Fillmore followed her. "How's her hard mouth coming along?" Cash asked. "Been able to do anything about it?"

Uncle Jesse and Skeeter swapped glances and the boy went in the cabin and got an egg and brought it out and put it on the ground. Then he whistled for Lady and she came to him and he nodded toward the egg and said, "Bring it here, Lady."

She tilted her face up to him and chuckled and looked over at Millard Fillmore and did not chuckle, and then she walked to the egg and took it gently into her mouth and brought it to the boy and there was no mark on it, not even a scratch.

Uncle Jesse r'ared back and strutted and Mister Cash's eyes bulged his surprise. "Egg toting!" he exclaimed. "Mouth soft as eiderdown." He did not spare his praise and stooped and patted Lady and she ran out her tongue at him and chuckled again.

"She does pretty good," Skeeter said modestly.

"Your dog do that, Cash?" Uncle Jesse was grinning. "Your dog egg tote?"

The storekeeper was taking no chances. "Ain't no use of wasting eggs. That's the trouble with you, Jesse. Always wasting things like eggs and such."

"It ain't wasted. Me and the boy will eat it."

Skeeter sensed an argument coming and moved to head it off. "Let's get going. I wasn't trying to show off, Mister Cash. Just wanted you know that my dog can egg tote. She won't bruise birds when real hunting time comes." He waited for Uncle Jesse to lead the way, as was fitting, and the old man moved out of the yard and the storekeeper was beside him, and Skeeter followed and the two dogs were close to him, that is, Lady was close to him and Millard Fillmore was as close to Lady as she would permit him to be.

They reached the ridges and high ground and Cash was sweating a bit around the band of his hat but Uncle Jesse was chilly and his nose was wet and his eyes were watery. He pulled his jumper collar tight around his neck and waited for Skeeter and the dogs to catch up and then they dropped down the ridge and into the broomstraw.

Cash called his dog and waved him out and Millard Fillmore glanced over his shoulder at Lady and raced into the brush and began casting. "Quick, ain't he?" Cash said.

"Cute all right." Uncle Jesse rammed his hands in his pockets. "Sharp as a briar. A merry tail, too—whipping right pert."

Skeeter waited until the big setter was deep in the sage and then he waved his hand and spoke gently to Lady. "Hup. Birds." She trotted across the field, chuckling as she went and her head came up and she took the breeze and wheeled and sprinted away, ripping through the broomstraw. Millard Fillmore was circling cautiously and surely, covering every inch of the ground, but Lady was whipping recklessly—racing around the big setter, working to the far edge of the field and then back again.

"She ain't casting," Cash said. "She's just running. She ought to stay close to ol' Mill and learn something."

"It's her way," Skeeter said.

"Can't no dog hunt that fast," Cash said. "You got to slow her down if you aim to make a bird dog out of her. She'll run herself out."

Millard Fillmore had worked to the edge of a pine thicket and was coming back slowly and Lady was out of sight. "Where you reckon she is?" Cash asked.

Skeeter climbed on a stump and looked around and couldn't see her.

"Bet she's plum' to Mobile by now," Cash said. "Running like that."

"She's on a point." Skeeter got down from the stump.

"What you mean—point?" Cash demanded. "How come you think she's on a point?"

"Because she ain't casting." The boy headed toward the pine thicket and the clearing beyond. "If she was running, we'd see her. And if she ain't running, she's standing still. And if she's standing still, she's got birds."

The storekeeper looked over at Uncle Jesse and winked and the three of them hurried toward the clearing and there was Lady standing cold still, her front legs spraddled and her tail stiff over her back like a poker.

"You call that a point?" Cash studied the dog closely and looked back over his shoulder at his own dog that still was circling. "That ain't no point. That's a squat."

"She's got birds," Skeeter said.

"Where? That clearing's as slick as a skillet. Where she got birds?"

Uncle Jesse leaned against a tree and had nothing to say and left everything to the boy and Skeeter pointed toward a clump of sage at the far side of the clearing. "Over yonder. That's where her birds are."

Cash Evans almost busted out laughing, but restrained himself because he must not hurt the boy's feelings. "Now, wait a minute. It's fifty—sixty yards to that sage. Can't no dog smell birds that far. Can't smell a polecat that far."

Just then Millard Fillmore ran by them and then by Lady and she did not budge, only crouching a bit lower. "He ran right by her," Skeeter said and there was accusation in his voice. "He ought'n have done that. He ought'a honored her point and backed her up. That's fit'n and proper."

"She ain't on no point." Cash was quick to defend his dog. "Ol' Mill would honor her point, but she ain't got no birds and he's still casting."

Millard Fillmore circled the clearing and then stopped and looked at Lady, and still she held fast, and so he began circling again, working toward the sage and then he caught the wind and stiffened to a point. It was perfect; his right leg up, his nose steady and his tail out straight. It was so beautiful and so perfect that Cash took off his hat, as though in tribute, and ran his sleeve across his forehead where a few beads of perspiration had formed in spite of the chilly weather. "Now there's a point."

"He ran right by my dog." Skeeter said it again. "He didn't honor her. He didn't back her up."

Uncle Jesse moved from his slouch against the tree and stepped close to Cash. "Your dog's pinting all right. Pretty as I ever seen. But where the birds?"

"They're out there. I'll flush 'em. Wish the season was on and I had my gun. Ol' Mill's got a covey."

"He sure has," Uncle Jesse said. "He's got Lady's covey."

That was an aspersion on the big setter, a slur at his breeding and behavior and Cash's face reddened in anger. "Don't stand there saying my dog sneaked another dog's covey."

"Keep your shirt on." Uncle Jesse was as calm as you please. "Ain't low-rating your dog. He's fit'n and mannerable but he just can't smell as good as Lady—"

"Whatcha saying, man? You gone crazy? Ol' Mill is a bird dog and that thing of yours is a hound. You gone crazy?"

Uncle Jesse ran his hand across his chin, rasping the white stubble there, and took his own slow time in answering and then he said deliberately, "There're quail in that sage. The boy's dog pinted 'em first and she's still pinting 'em. Your dog can't smell as good as her and that's how come he ran by her. He got close enough to smell them birds and went on his point. He's still on it, pinting the same birds that Lady's been pinting all along."

"Prove it!" Cash Evans was splutteringly mad. "You've thow'd your bait and so back it up, or back down."

"For the saw?"

"You mighty come a'right for the saw. You doggone tooting for the saw and for all the groceries you can tote—"

"Ain't pushing it." Uncle Jesse picked up a pine cone and tossed it up and down. "Just laying that saw against double what I owe you. So fish or cut bait, Brother Evans. Shoot or give up the gun. Call or crawl."

"I don't yell calf rope, Jesse Jackson, and you know that good as me. The saw's on the line and I'm standing you that the boy's dog ain't got birds."

Uncle Jesse tossed the pine cone to Skeeter. "Go flush the covey. They're in that sage like Lady been telling us all along."

The boy walked by his dog, treading lightly, and her eyes followed him but she did not move, and then he walked by Millard Fillmore and the big setter did not move either, and then he was close to the sage and he threw the pine cone into the covering.

The covey flew up, whirring frantically, and bunched

tight and flashed away. Lady broke her point and sat on her haunches and ran out her tongue and laughed, but Millard Fillmore held his point for a few more seconds as though all of this could not be true and then he turned his head and looked back at Lady and then he slunk away, his head low and his tail dragging.

Cash Evans was dumbfounded and his little eyes blinked slowly and his lips quivered. Uncle Jesse slouched against the tree again and Skeeter came back and joined them and felt sorry for Mister Cash, and then the storekeeper spoke and there was a catch in his voice. "I'm going home."

Skeeter shoved his hands deep in his pockets and went over and slouched against the tree by Uncle Jesse and said nothing, knowing that nothing he could say would lessen Mister Cash's humiliation. Millard Fillmore was in the pine thicket, alone and dejected, and kept watching his master, expecting a rebuke or maybe sympathy—or anything, just something; some word of some sort. Lady looked his way only once and then walked across the clearing and to Skeeter's side and stood by him in majestic arrogance. She had humbled a dog that once had been too good to work with her and now she was rubbing it in. The boy wished she wouldn't do like that, but there was no way for him to tell her. He could teach her to hunt and to come to him and to fetch things, but he couldn't teach her to forgive. After all, she was just a dog and no one can expect dogs to act like people.

Mister Cash fumbled for his pipe but had no tobacco with him and Uncle Jesse offered his pouch and held a match for his friend to get a light. Cash thanked him and then said, "You got yourself a saw."

"No hard feelings, Cash."

"No hard feelings. Now I'll be going home."

"Maybe you'll stop by our place for a cup of coffee."

"I'll be going home. When I see a hound dog that can laugh and point birds fifty yards away—well, I've had enough."

He started away and then he stopped and looked over toward the pines and again his lips quivered and he called out, "Come on, Mill. Come on. Let's me and you go home."

The big dog bounded out of the thicket and Cash squatted on the ground and held out his arms and his dog ran to him and whimpered and licked his face. Cash stroked him very gently and again the humbled one looked over at Lady and she raised her head even higher and then turned her head away in haughty disdain.

"Got me a good dog, though." Cash said it in fierce pride.

"He's a good dog," Skeeter said gravely.

"A mighty good dog." Uncle Jesse said it gravely, too.

"It's just that when you think you got the best, som'n better always comes along." The storekeeper sucked deep on his pipe and blew the smoke into the chilly air and then he told Uncle Jesse and Skeeter so long, but said nothing to Lady. Not a word.

CHAPTER ∽ ∽ ∽ ∽ NINE

THE WORD GOT AROUND THAT THE OLD MAN AND THE boy had a laughing dog that pointed quail at fifty yards and folks came from up and down the river to gawk at Lady; and they fed her tidbits like she was something in a zoo and brought gifts to Uncle Jesse and Skeeter for the privilege of seeing the marvel.

They brought hams and bacon sidings and buckets of molasses and pickled peaches and soon the shelf by the stove was laden with good things and the corner by the back door was filled with presents: fat kindling wood already cut, big red sweet potatoes and four sacks of hickory nuts.

Uncle Jesse took to sitting in a rocker on the front porch on pretty days and meeting the folks and telling them all about the dog. He had a sort of sing-song spiel that he said over and over to the curious who gathered in the yard and shook their heads in wonderment or in doubt, or nodded in agreement and thus indicated that they were wise and had seen many strange things before and that nothing surprised them.

"Now, I'm sitting right here in this rocker and telling you—" That's the way he began. "Know you won't believe it, but seeing's believing as the old saying goes. The boy found her in the swamp and she can't bark a'tall. Just laughs. Beaten'st thing you ever seen."

The visitors talked to him about it all and listened to him and went away talking about him, and toothless old Jesse Jackson was somebody at last.

Lady herself quickly associated the strangers with the tidbits they brought and she learned to sit up and beg and catch the choice morsels the folks threw to her and no longer did she relish the oatmeal and bacon drippings that the old man and the boy shared with her.

Skeeter enjoyed it all almost as much as Uncle Jesse and even more than Lady and when he saw folks coming up the road he always ran to the old man and hollered, "Get set. Here come some more."

Then Uncle Jesse wet his fingers on his tongue and smoothed down his hair and went to the front porch and sat in the rocker. Lady dashed to the front steps

and was ready to sit up and catch the tidbits, and
Skeeter waited by the side of the cabin until Uncle Jesse
had had his say and Lady had collected her contribu-
tions and then he whistled and Lady went to him, and
the folks followed her.

"Now laugh." He always said it loud enough for the
folks to hear and his dog tilted her head and chuckled.

He gave them time to express their amazement and
for the skeptics to come close and then he said, "Now
cry."

She did, and again he let the skeptics come close so
they could see the tears in her eyes.

"Ain't that the beaten'st thing you ever seen?" Uncle
Jesse called out from his rocker and the folks agreed it
was the beaten'st thing they'd ever seen.

Sometimes, if they still doubted, Skeeter took them
back across the ridges and let them see his dog work
the fields and point at fifty yards; and nothing had happened to cause so much talk in the swamp since the big
freeze of '17 and that was a long time before Skeeter
was born.

The autumn was wasting and the hard, brittle winter
was fast upon the swamp and the boy knew it was high
time for him to break his dog to the gun and kill quail
and let her fetch them and be a real bird dog instead
of just a show dog. He mentioned it several times to

Uncle Jesse and the old man agreed that her training should be resumed, but every time Skeeter made up his mind to take her out the next day and shoot over her and correct any faults if she were gun shy—well, every time he got all set to do what he knew he ought to do then five or six folks always dropped by and on every day except Sunday and it wouldn't be right for him to hunt on Sunday.

This was the state of things when Cash Evans drove out and just sort of hung around and didn't say much of anything and Uncle Jesse sensed that he wanted to talk to him alone, and so he sent Skeeter down to the spring for a fresh bucket of water and then he said, "What's on your mind, Cash? What's eatin' you?"

"Nothing's eatin' me. Just dropped by." His manner was heavy, however, and he was without spirit and was fidgety. He waited until Skeeter was out of sight and went over to the stack of magazines and began sorting them and holding each one up to the afternoon light that drifted through the window.

"You ain't fooling nobody," Uncle Jesse said. "Som'n eatin' you bad."

Cash glared down at the magazines and at Uncle Jesse, and went over and sat at the table and stroked his bald head. "Got to tell you. You'll find out anyway."

"Tell me what? Quit beating around the stump."

"Well, now, that dog is causing a heap of talk around here. Maybe I started it. Told some of the folks around the store what I had seen and so maybe I started it, but I didn't go to do it."

"Quit beating around the stump, like I said. What's on your mind?"

"Well, now, a fellow was out from Mobile about a week ago to sell me some stuff and he heard the folks in the store talking about that dog."

"Everybody's talking about her. Beaten'st thing you ever seen."

"That fellow was back out this morning to sell me some more stuff and he brought me a clipping out of a magazine." Cash felt in his pocket and held the clipping up to the light and looked at it and then passed it to Uncle Jesse.

The old man also looked at it and then passed it back. "It's rightly nice of you to show it to me just like I could read. You always been mighty nice about it, Cash. Mighty nice. But the boy ain't here and so I'll have to bother you to read it to me. Or tell me what it says."

"I ain't enjoying this, Jesse. Just want you to know that."

"Plain as day you ain't, but I'm listening. What it say?"

"It's about a breed of dogs. Basenji—that's the breed. Live in Africa."

"You don't say."

"Just about the oldest breed there is. Go way back before our-Lord-and-Savior-Jesus-Christ. Way back before Moses even."

"That old, huh?"

"Older'n that. Still a few of 'em in Africa. Best hunting dogs in the world."

"Lady?"

"Uh huh."

"How you know?"

"Them dogs can't bark. Laugh when they try to bark. Stand about so high—" He held out his hand and it was Lady's height. "Red and silky and a blaze on the chest. Lick themselves like cats."

"Sounds like Lady all right."

"It's Lady, Jesse. Sure as shooting, she's one of them dogs."

"Then how come her 'way over here?"

"Working up to that. So don't shove me."

"I ain't shoving."

The storekeeper folded the clipping and returned it to his pocket and then took a match out of his pocket and broke it and used it to clean his fingernails; and he was silent for a bit and then he said: "That fellow from

Mobile brought a magazine out with him this morning. Hunting magazine, and the minute I seen it I remembered seeing it before. The picture on the front—that's how I recollected. It's the same magazine that I brought out here a few months back."

"Then it's still here. What does it look like? I'll find it." The old man moved over to the pile of magazines.

"Got a picture of a goat on the front. Big goat with horns that go ever' whichaway. And a fellow with a .30-.30."

"It's here som'rs." Uncle Jesse riffled through the magazines until he found the one with the mountain goat on the cover and he handed it to Cash.

Methodically, almost painfully, the storekeeper wet his finger and thumbed through the magazine until he found what he was looking for and he held it up to the window light. "It's a ad. 'Way back in the back." And then he read.

"Lost—a Basenji female in the vicinity of Pascagoula swamp in Mississippi. Twenty-two inches high. White blaze on chest and white collar. Answers to name of Isis of the Blue Nile. Liberal reward for recovery. Old Brook Kennels. Old Lyme, Connecticut."

He stumbled on the word *Basenji* and on *Isis* and slurred the word *Connecticut* and then he looked up and Uncle Jesse's chin was drooped to his chest and he was gazing at the floor and seeing nothing. There was a long silence and Uncle Jesse raised his head and looked off toward the swamp and then he said, "Ain't that a pretty name—Isis of the Blue Nile. Never heard a name like that."

"What's that got to do with it?" Cash rolled the magazine and poked it under his arm. "They talking about the boy's dog."

"Know it. Know'n it right off. Just wanted to put off thinking about it."

"The boy'll be back t'reckly. I'll get going and take this magazine along. He'll never know the difference."

"You mean don't tell him?"

"You mean you aim to tell him?"

"He'll find out. All those folks flocking here—somebody'll hear about it and tell him." Uncle Jesse walked over to the fireplace and kicked one of the blazing logs and sparks showered and then he rested his arm on the mantel. "There's a reward and somebody will go after that reward. He'll find out, so it's right for me to tell him."

"It's your load."

"I'll tote it."

"But if it was me, I wouldn't tell him." Cash took the magazine from under his arm and rolled it tighter and stuck it back under his arm. "That dog is the only thing the boy ever called his'n. No, I wouldn't tell him. I'd let things lay."

"That's you and I'm me, Cash. You know how to run a store and how to train bird dogs, but me—I got to raise a young'un. So I'll tell him."

"Like I said, it's your load."

"Like I said, I'll tote it."

Cash buttoned his jacket tight and reached for his hat. "Then I'll be going." He tossed the magazine back on the pile. "I'm saying again—I ain't enjoying this."

He put on his hat and Uncle Jesse went out to the truck with him and then he was gone and Uncle Jesse went back to the fire and pulled a chair close to the hearth and sat down and waited. He heard Skeeter and Lady on the front steps and heard the boy put the water bucket in its proper place and then the boy and the dog were in the cabin and it was full.

Skeeter went over to the fire and held his hands over the blaze and Lady went over to his bed and curled on it and Uncle Jesse said nothing, just staring at the fire and wondering how he would tell it.

"What's eatin' Mister Cash?" Skeeter stood before the fire and held his hands behind him. "Acted put out, like som'n buzzing round him."

"Som'n you got to know." Uncle Jesse could not figure a way to back into the matter. "Som'n I got to tell you."

"Lady?" The boy reacted intuitively.

The old man nodded and picked up the magazine and wished he could find the place, but all the words looked alike and so he handed the magazine to the boy. "Over at the back. One of them ads. About a lost dog."

Skeeter found the ad and read it, mumbling the words half aloud and stumbling on the big ones; and Uncle Jesse watched his face and there was no change in the boy's expression and he read the notice again and closed the magazine and looked a long time at the picture on the front. "Isis of the Blue Nile," he said. "That's a funny name. Wonder what they called her? Bet they called her Blue for short."

"They talking about Lady," Uncle Jesse said.

"Never heard of a dog like that. Basenji. Just never heard of a dog like that."

"Come from Africa."

"How you know?"

"Cash told me. And he sure hated to tell me."

"Then how come he told you?"

"Sort of trapped him. Had to tell me."

"I see."

"Had to tell me like I had to tell you. And it's Lady all right."

188

"Ain't saying it ain't." The boy's expression changed then and his jaw drooped slightly and trembled. "Just saying I never heard of a dog like that."

Uncle Jesse jerked a splinter from one of the blazing logs and lit his pipe and the cabin was quiet. "Dogs like that been in Africa a long time. Back before our-Lord-and-Savior-Jesus-Christ. Before Moses, even. They can't bark."

"How you know?"

"Cash told me."

"How he know?"

"Fellow from Mobile told him. Travelling man."

"I see." The boy blinked his eyes rapidly and turned from his uncle and looked across the room at Lady, and then turned from her. Neither of them must see him, for he was too big to cry and so they mustn't see him. "If it's my dog and she belongs in Africa—well, what she doing here?"

Uncle Jesse's pipe tasted bitter and he put it on the mantel. "Somebody brought her over. Maybe them folks in the ad. Brought her over and she got lost. That's about how it happened."

"Well, I found her." The boy's eyes were dry and he faced his uncle and the line of his mouth was straight. "I found her and finder's keepers."

189

"That's the saying all right and some folks hold to that."

"How you hold?"

"I ain't holding. You're doing the holding."

"But what you think I ought to do, Uncle Jesse?" His jaw was trembling again. "I don't know what to do. What you think I ought to do?"

The old man pulled his chair closer to the fire and sat down again and held his long gnarled hands out to the blaze and again the cabin was quiet, and evening gloom was creeping down from the ridges and over the cabin and into the swamp. "Well, now—I rightly don't know. You can keep still about that dog and nothing mout never happen. Then again a heap of folks know about her and somebody mout put two and two together. There's always that reward."

"Mister Cash?"

"Never in this world. Cash Evans loves money as good as the next man, but not that good. So like I said, nothing mout never happen. But then again it mout. This one you got to settle for yourself."

"But I don't know how."

"Me neither. But whichever way you jump, I'm jumping with you."

"If I keep her then that's all right with you?"

"If you think it's right to lay low and keep her, then

it's you and me and the dog and ain't nothing going to bother you. They can bring the high sheriff. The governor even. It don't make no difference. Ain't nobody going to bother you. Ain't nobody going to take no dog away from nobody unless that's how you want it."

"Then I'm going to keep her."

The old man got up from his chair and picked up his pipe and blew into it and got a broomstraw and cleaned it. "If that's how it is, then let's fix some supper. A big bowl of oatmeal sounds good to me. How 'bout you?"

"Maybe those folks forgot about her by now. That's an old magazine and she been lost a long time."

"Some hot oatmeal and maybe some ham all chopped up in some eggs." Uncle Jesse went over to the stove and lit some splinters.

"Mor'n likely those folks have forgot all about her." The boy reached for the oatmeal and a porringer and handed them to Uncle Jesse.

"If we have oatmeal for supper, we better have mush for breakfast. Don't want to overdo the oatmeal." The fire was burning good and the old man lifted an eye from the stove and put the porringer close to the blaze.

"Nobody around here much reads magazines except Mister Cash and Gates. That travelling man may not be back for months. So I'm going to keep her."

"You said that once't. Ain't no use keep talking about

it. Chop up the ham. Chop it into little bitty pieces so I can chew it."

The boy got the ham and sliced off a piece and cut it into little bitty pieces and then he got four eggs and broke them and mixed the ham with the eggs, but his eyes had filled again and he didn't look up; and finally he said, "Uncle Jesse—"

"Uh huh?"

"I ain't hungry."

"You oughta eat."

"But I ain't hungry." He turned away from the stove and went over to the front door and stood there and Lady jumped off of the bed and joined him and they went out on the porch and then into the yard.

Uncle Jesse kept right on fixing supper and said nothing at all to the boy, and did not even look his way when he walked from the porch and into the yard.

Skeeter sauntered around the side of the cabin, wandering aimlessly and Lady stayed close to him and watched him, and then he swung away from the cabin and down the path toward the swamp. Twilight was melting into the first drift of dark and the shadows floated heavy across the swamp, and the early night things ventured out and began calling.

The boy sat on a stump and his dog put her head on his leg. "Isis of the Blue Nile." He said it harshly, hoping that she would refuse the name.

But she didn't. Her ears came up and she cocked her head and looked at him.

"You know it. You know it all right."

Then there were tears in her eyes and she moved as close to him as she could get and she drooped her head.

"But you don't like it."

He reached down and picked her up and she licked his face and his neck and began chuckling. "Don't you worry," he said softly. "Ain't nothing going to bother you."

His words gave him courage and he felt better, but only for a minute and then the conflict was back within him; the tyranny of a boy's conscience.

"Once I found a Barlow knife and kept it and it was all right." He mumbled it to his conscience.

But this is different, Skeeter. You know it's different and, besides, you'll get caught up with.

"Finders, keepers; losers, weepers."

No, Skeeter. Suppose you had lost the dog and they had found her.

"Well, I don't care. She's mine."

She'll never be yours. Not really yours.

A feeling of despair and loneliness almost overwhelmed him. He fought off the tears as long as he could but finally he gave in and his sobs brought Lady closer to him and she peered into his face and wondered why he was behaving so strangely when they were together, and then she wept too because he was weeping. He put his arms around her and opened the flood gates of his misery. "My li'l old puppy dog. Poor li'l old puppy dog. But we got to do it."

He sniffed back his tears and got up and the twilight was gone and the swamp was night black, and teeming and squirming. "We got to do it. And, besides, we'd get caught up with. They'd find out." The door to the cabin still was open and the light from the fireplace was yellow through the doorway and very warm and soothing, and he saw Uncle Jesse moving about; and he started running back toward the cabin and he ran very fast as though he feared he might lose that too; the place and Uncle Jesse and everything. He slowed down when he got to the steps and he was relieved and comforted to find them firm and safe to his tread, and he and Lady went back inside.

"Uncle Jesse—"

"I'm listening." The old man lifted the porringer of oatmeal and filled the bowls.

"Know what I aim to do?"

"Uh huh."

"What you think I aim to do?"

194

"Get word to them folks up yonder that you got their dog."

"How'd you know? How'd you know that?"

"Just knew. Now, sit down and eat your supper."

"Ain't hungry. And we got to do it, ain't we?"

"Like I said before, you doing the holding. It's your load and you got to tote it."

"Aim to tote it. But don't know how to get in touch with those folks. Way up yonder."

"Just write 'em a letter."

"Letter take a long time. Want to get shed of it. Since I got to do it, I want to do it quick."

"Then maybe a telegram."

"But don't know nothing about a telegram. Don't know how to send one."

"Me neither. But Cash'll know."

"Don't want Mister Cash in it."

"Don't be hard on Cash. He couldn't help it."

"Gates'll know. Gates knows about things like that. I'm going over and see Gates."

"Right now?"

"Soon as you get through your supper."

"I ain't hungry neither." Uncle Jesse took the lamp from the table and put it over by his bed and looked around for his jacket. "Come to think about it I ain't hungry even a frazzling bit."

Skeeter lit the lantern and Lady came over to him and Skeeter said, "You stay here and watch things. Be back t'reckly."

He put on his jacket and picked up the magazine and Lady followed them to the front porch and sat on the steps and they walked away toward the bayou. Uncle Jesse walked ahead and held the lantern high. There was neither moon nor stars that night and the night was very dark.

A slush of rain water was in the bottom of the skiff but not enough to bother with and bail out and Uncle Jesse was climbing in the skiff when they heard the noise up ahead and they looked at each other quickly and were still.

" 'Gator?" the boy whispered.

"Too loud for a 'gator. Somebody fishing, mor'n likely. Catfish running and it'll be some of them Watsons, mor'n likely. Maybe even Gates hisself." Uncle Jesse cupped his hands and called out, "Who's that? Down the bayou? This here is Jesse Jackson."

"It's me—Gates Watson." The voice came back deep from the swamp and echoing.

"Like I figured," Uncle Jesse said and climbed back out of the skiff. "Catfish running."

They walked down the bayou and found Gates at the mouth of the stream, where it emptied into the river,

196

and he was setting out trot-lines, stringing the lines across the bayou and baiting the gang hooks with fat meat and biscuit dough.

"On our way over to your place." Uncle Jesse put the lantern on a log and squatted by it.

"What's wrong?" Gates looked from the old man to the boy. Something was bound to be wrong—swamp folks going visiting this time of night.

"It's Lady." Skeeter opened the magazine and stooped by the lantern and found the place and handed the magazine to Gates.

He scarcely glanced at it and handed it back and bent over his trot-lines again. "One of those fancy kennels. Way up there." He jerked a slipknot in one of his lines as though he was angry at something, perhaps just at the way things happen. "You telling, Claude? You telling them you found her?"

"Got to. She ain't mine so I'm bound to tell 'em."

"That's how come we were going to your place." Uncle Jesse felt for his pipe and had left it at the cabin. "Aim to send a telegram, but me and the boy ain't never sent a telegram before."

"Figured you'd help us," Skeeter said. "Help us write it out and me and Uncle Jesse could go to Pascagoula tomorrow and send it."

Gates foresaw the complications and knew that he

must be discreet. He fumbled with his lines as he turned things in his mind and then he said, "Like you know, telegrams are sent on a special kind of paper that you get at the Western Union office."

"We know that," Uncle Jesse said quickly. "Everybody knows that."

"It's just that me and Uncle Jesse ain't never up and sent one," Skeeter said. "We gen'ly write letters, but a letter take too long this time."

"Take a long time all right," Gates said. "Way up there."

"So me and Uncle Jesse figured we could go over to your house and write it down." Skeeter met the issue with tact, and yet forthrightly. "Then me and Uncle Jesse would take it in town tomorrow and copy it right."

"If that's how you want to do it, we'll go write it out." Gates reached down for his flashlight and put it in his pocket.

Then the enormity of their problem came to the boy and to the old man and they looked quickly at each other and realized how helpless they were. It would never do for the boy to copy the telegram in a public place while the old man was there. It would be the old man's place to do the writing and because he couldn't—then folks would know. Skeeter could go in by himself and that might work out, but he was terrified at the thought of facing the intricacies of sending a telegram alone. There was no word between the boy and the old man, only that look of helplessness between them, and yet each knew what the other was thinking.

So did Gates. He dug in his pocket for his cigarettes and offered one to Uncle Jesse and the old man refused politely and then Gates said, "I'll be going into Pascagoula tomorrow. I'll send it, if you want me to."

"You going anyway?" Skeeter said. "Me and Uncle Jesse don't aim to put you to no trouble."

"I'm going anyway. It won't be any trouble."

"You'll do it right, now, Gates." The sag went out of Uncle Jesse's shoulders and he straightened them. "You sure you know how to do it?"

"I'll fix it."

"Just walk in there big as you please," Uncle Jesse instructed. "Just tell 'em you aim to send a telegram for Jesse Jackson and his nephew. About a dog. Then write it out pretty. You'll be signing the boy's name, so do it good. Do it myself, but ain't no use double-teaming if you're going in anyhow."

"You can count on it, Mr. Jesse."

"Now what you going to tell 'em?"

"That their Basenji has been found and where it is. That's all."

"That's the ticket," Uncle Jesse said. "That's the way to do it."

The boy looked up from the lantern into the face of his friend and his eyes widened in the knowledge of a truth. "Wait a minute, Gates. You knew about Lady. It just hit me. You knew about her all along."

"What makes you say that?"

"The way you said that name. You didn't even study that magazine, but you just come out with that name easy as you please. You ain't that smart. Ain't nobody that smart."

"Basenji?" Gates was embarrassed. Most men might have been proud that they knew more than their neighbors, but not Gates Watson because he was a shy man and reticent, and had been away to school and that made him different from all the others.

"You knew about that dog?" Uncle Jesse demanded authoritatively.

"In a way, I suppose I did. Since you put it that way, it's up to me—well, I figured right off that she was a Basenji and mighty valuable."

Skeeter stepped back into the shadows, but Uncle Jesse pressed the point. "How'd you know? Mr. Evans didn't know and I didn't know, so how'd you know?"

"I heard her in the swamp about the time you folks did, Mr. Jesse. Then I saw her and knew that she didn't belong around here. A dog that couldn't bark. A dog that laughed. So I read up on it."

"Did you try to catch her?"

"Yes, sir. I knew she was worth a lot of money."

"Why didn't you tell me, Gates?" Skeeter spoke from the shadows. "How come you let me play like she was mine?"

"I just did, that's all." Gates dropped his cigarette by the lantern and ground it out. "I was down by the spring looking for her the day you found her. I'd put out baits, but she wouldn't come to me. I saw her go to you and that's all there is to it."

"Should have told me. Wouldn't have been so hard to give her up at first."

"I wish now that I had. But I just couldn't, Claude. You had yourself a dog and I just couldn't throw you."

"You let me think she was mine and you knew better all the time. You should have told me, Gates." He turned away from both of them and started for home.

Uncle Jesse and Gates remained there by the lantern and finally Gates said, "He's put out with me. I don't want Claude mad at me. But I just couldn't tell him."

"He'll get over it. Don't you get down in the mouth, Gates. You done right and he'll get over it."

"But he's aching, Mr. Jesse. I never saw anybody aching so hard."

"All dry inside," Uncle Jesse said. "Like a water well dug deep and then run dry." He picked up the lantern and told Gates good night and walked fast and caught up with the boy and they went home together.

The fire had died to embers and Uncle Jesse's bed was cold, but the boy's was warm because his dog had slept there while he was gone.

CHAPTER ~ ~ ~ ~ TEN

THE MAN FROM THE KENNEL WAS NAMED WALDEN
Grover and he flew down to Mobile and rented a truck
and drove out to the swamp. Skeeter and Lady were not
at home and Uncle Jesse was surprised that the man
showed up so quick and was a little bit in awe of anybody who had flown in an airplane.

He asked the stranger in, but Mr. Grover was distant
at first and ill at ease and he stood at the steps and
wanted to know all about the Basenji and when he
could pick her up. "Is she in good shape?" he said.

"Slick as el'um," Uncle Jesse said. "She and the boy
went across the river to the Watsons. That's a colored
family and finer folks as you ever seen. We get milk
from 'em, and the boy took his dog and went over there

a little while ago—"

"How's she eating? She's a very valuable dog." Mr. Grover almost was embarrassed in the old man's presence and didn't know why. He glanced around at the bare yard, at the ground so hard and the house so drab. He had heard and had read much about such folks as Uncle Jesse, the red-necks, the pecker-woods, and he wanted to get this over with and be away from there.

Uncle Jesse looked down from the porch at the visitor and slouched against the post that supported the roof over the porch. "She been eatin' same stuff as us. Oatmeal and bacon fat and things like that."

Mr. Grover cringed inside of himself and grimaced. Dogs were his business. "A valuable dog like that should have meat once a day."

"Well, now, I do declare." Uncle Jesse moved over to the steps and sat down and leaned against the post and crossed his long legs. "Meat every day, huh? And here we been giving her the same sort of stuff we eat." He looked at Mr. Grover's whipcord breeches and his freshly shaved face and the tiny blue veins in his cheeks. He had never met a man like this before and was impressed and, like all the lonely ones of the world, he wanted to know him better and learn about him and share the full measure of this experience; something new and something so different. "The boy and the dog'll be back t'reckly. Why don't you come in and sit awhile. Take the rocker." He nodded toward the rocking chair there on the porch.

"I am anxious to get back to Mobile. I can get a plane back home tonight."

"Way back up there, huh? Me, I never been way up there. Been over to Louisiana, though. Almost went to Texas once't. You ever been over there? Louisiana and Texas?"

Mr. Grover said that he had been to Louisiana and Texas and some of the impatience went out of his tone. "I don't want to hurry you, but I've come a long way for that dog."

"You sure have. And what did you say your name was?"

"I didn't say. But it is Grover."

"First or last?"

"Last. My name is Walden Grover." The visitor moved closer to the steps and hesitated a second and then sat down. Can't hurry these folks. He'd always heard that. Time had no meaning to them and he might as well make the best of the situation.

"Mr. Grover, huh?" Uncle Jesse never had seen whip-cord breeches before and wanted to ask about them, but this man didn't invite conversation. In a hurry, too.

Some folks always in a hurry. "Any kin to Grover Cleveland?"

"Grover Cleveland?" The visitor looked up quickly at the old man and smiled and hoped that the old man would not misunderstand the smile, as though anyone could. "No, no kin."

"He was President of the United States," Uncle Jesse said. "Used to hear a lot about him when I was a boy. Came from up your way and so I thought maybe you might be kin, sort of."

Mr. Grover stood up again and brushed off his breeches and obviously was wondering about the dog. "We thought we would hear about that Basenji long before we did. She was lost months ago. We advertised in magazines and newspapers."

Uncle Jesse looked away from the tiny blue veins in the man's face and toward the swamp. "We just found out about her. That she belonged to you, I mean. The boy found her in the swamp and she took to him and just a few days ago we seen your ad in an old magazine. Cash Evans was in on it. He runs the store down in Lystra; that little crossroad town you come through. Ol' Cash is a mighty fine man and was mighty down in the mouth that he was in on letting the boy know that the dog belonged to somebody else."

"If the reward is not large enough—" Mr. Grover

fidgeted and took out a package of cigarettes and offered one to Uncle Jesse and the old man took it although he didn't smoke cigarettes, but Gates Watson did and he might as well take it and give it to Gates.

"Reward?" Uncle Jesse rolled the cigarette between his fingers and then put it away. "I'd forgot about the reward. Remember now, though, that that magazine did say som'n about it."

Mr. Grover was skeptical of this sort of talk and quickly was on his guard. "I only work for the kennel. I don't own it. But I have been authorized to pay a $50 reward. That's a lot of money."

He had been authorized to pay a $100 reward and if that were not acceptable he was to hire an attorney and recover the dog by law. But if he could save his employer money, then that would be fine. Fifty dollars was a big sum to these people. He was thinking they never had seen $50 at one time, and he was right. And so he said it again. "It's a lot of money. I'll pay as soon as I get the dog. Of course, I don't want any trouble, but the dog legally belongs to us."

Uncle Jesse got up slowly and again he slouched against the post and was baffled and looked a long time at the stranger. "Trouble? Won't be no trouble, Mr. Grover. Soon as the boy gets back—well, you'll get your dog."

"I'll pay the money to you. It's a lot of money to give a boy."

"That's between you and him." Uncle Jesse still was baffled and took off his hat and ran his long finger around the sweatband and turned things in his mind. This fellow sure was hard to get next to, sure was hard to talk to. "The boy found the dog and it's his business. And me—well, I don't like this trouble talk."

"No offense." Some of the crispness went out of Mr. Grover's voice. "I just thought perhaps you might not want to give up the dog."

"Don't. But she's yours."

"Naturally, I hate to take a dog away from a boy—"

"Now, hold on a minute." Uncle Jesse straightened from his slouch. "Ain't nobody taking nothing from nobody. The boy found your dog and she's yours, but ain't nobody taking nothing from nobody."

"I didn't mean it that way," Mr. Grover blurted out. It looked like everything he said was said the wrong way and he was on the defensive and there was no reason for him to be on the defensive. He rested one foot on the steps and looked steadily up at the old man. "I don't like this any more than you do—coming down here like this. How would you feel if you were in my shoes—coming down here to take a dog away from a boy?"

"I wouldn't like it." The lines around Uncle Jesse's mouth drooped and he was sad, and he was sorry that he had spoken hard to the visitor. The man was just doing the best he could; they were all just doing the best they could. "We both a bit touchy," Uncle Jesse said. "Why don't you come on in and I'll build up the fire and we'll have a cup of coffee. The boy'll be back t'reckly and ain't no use of me and you standing out here and having a go-round."

Mr. Grover went into the cabin and Uncle Jesse threw a pine knot on the fire and the fire blazed bright and then he took the coffeepot off of the stove and put it on the hearth to warm it up. He pulled a chair close to the fire and Mr. Grover sat down and glanced around, and the spell of the place was upon him; the solitude and the abiding loneliness.

Uncle Jesse stood by the mantel and lit his pipe. "Ain't much, but it's ours. Mine and the boy's."

"I've never been in a house like this before," the visitor said and he was no longer a stranger because a man must not be a stranger in another man's home. "I've seen them, but I've never been in one before."

"It'll do." Uncle Jesse drew deep on his pipe. "Sort of crowded, though. Some day I aim to add another room. Going right out and cut some logs and add another room. For the boy. He needs another room."

"You both sleep and eat in here?"

"Uh huh. The boy sleeps over yonder in that bed and the dog right next. You know how it is with a boy and a dog."

"Yes, I know."

Uncle Jesse stooped and felt the coffeepot and it was getting warm. "The trouble with boys is that they grow up."

Mr. Grover nodded slowly and he wanted to be away from this place because its spell was on him and he knew that it would haunt him forever, an old man and a boy and a dog, and he must break it; he must take the dog away and leave an empty place in this cabin. He tried not to think about it and began talking about his own home and his tongue was loosed and he talked a lot, more than he had ever talked before to a man he didn't know at all.

Uncle Jesse just stood there nodding and watching him and then the coffee was warm and Uncle Jesse filled two cups and they drank together.

"Don't know what's keeping the boy." Uncle Jesse kicked the pine knot on the fire and it blazed higher and the cabin was hot and stuffy to Mr. Grover, and smelled of bacon grease and molasses and boy and dog.

"You don't suppose anything's happened to him?"

"He'll be back t'reckly. Mor'n likely he's just walk-

ing around the swamp, him and the dog. And just looking. You know how a boy is. Maybe you'll stay and
eat some dinner with us."

"I can't do that. I'd like to, Mr. Jackson, but I can't
do that. Perhaps we should go look for the boy."

"No, let's don't do that." Uncle Jesse knocked his
pipe against the mantel and the ashes spilled on the
hearth. "I wouldn't want to walk up on the boy, me
and you, and have to up and tell him that you'd come
for his dog. Just up and tell him like that. We weren't
expecting you for a few more days, and I wouldn't
want us to go looking for him and just up and tell him
right off."

"I feel the same way." Mr. Grover poured himself
another swallow of coffee and then put the empty cup
on the mantel. "But I want to be back in Mobile tonight."

"Then I tell you what. If you can't stay for dinner,
then me and the boy will meet you at Cash Evans'
store. You just drive back down the road to Lystra and
go to Mr. Alpheus Evans' store and general merchan-
dise and tell ol' Cash you're a friend of mine and wait
there, and me and the boy and the dog will be in just
as soon as he gets back."

"All right." Mr. Grover reached for his hat. "If that's
the way you want it then that's the way we'll do it. I

just want to get it over with."

Uncle Jesse walked out to the truck with him and hated to see him go because he was somebody new to talk to and with things new to talk about. Mr. Grover backed the truck around and Uncle Jesse called out to him that he sure did know how to back a truck good, and then Mr. Grover drove away; and he was no longer suspicious.

He went to Cash's store and introduced himself and asked if he might wait there and Cash told him to make himself at home and sold him a can of salmon and some cheese and crackers for lunch, and a bottle of pop.

He tried to talk to the storekeeper about Uncle Jesse and the boy and, at first, Cash was rightly shut-mouth and wouldn't open up at all because he thought the stranger was prying. Gradually, however, the barrier melted away and Cash told him all about Uncle Jesse and the boy, except, of course, he didn't tell him that the old man couldn't read or write. "Some folks say ol' Jesse Jackson ain't no-count. But I say it depends on how you look at things. Oh, he's lazy. Too lazy to brush flies. But he's raised that boy. And if he told you they'd bring the dog in, they'll bring it in. So you just sit down and take the load off your feet."

And so Mr. Grover waited and along about the middle of the afternoon Uncle Jesse and Skeeter walked into the store and Lady was with them.

The dog was sleek because Skeeter had washed her in the bayou and had fed her the best food in the cabin, and the boy was sleek, too, because Uncle Jesse had cut his hair and wet it down and parted it.

Mr. Grover glanced expertly at Lady and knew that she was in good shape and then looked closely at the boy and saw that there was no bitterness in Skeeter and that pleasured him. Cash was the first to speak. "Jesse, this here is Mr. Grover. You two done met."

"Howdied but ain't shook." Uncle Jesse offered his hand and then introduced Skeeter.

The boy shook hands man-like. It was natural for him to do so because he had never known how to be a child and had spent all of his years with men, with Uncle Jesse and Mister Cash and Gates Watson. "Sorry I was late," he said. "Didn't know you'd get here so soon and me and Lady were out in the swamp just messin' around. Here's your dog."

"She looks good." Mr. Grover tried to smile but his smile was fixed and without meaning. Then he swallowed the lump that was in his throat and spoke his feelings. "I'm sorry about this, son. In a way, I wish we'd never found out about her."

"Oh, that's all right. That's the way things are." Being a boy, he was a realist. Grownups are the sentimentalists. "I know'd all along I couldn't keep her. Know'd all along that something would happen."

Mr. Grover reached in his pocket and took out a roll of bills, the $100 that he had been authorized to pay and was mortified inside of himself that he'd ever thought of less. "This is the reward. You can count it."

"Ain't no use of that." Skeeter held the money in his hand and stared down at it and then at Lady. A ten dollar bill was on the outside of the roll and the boy never before even had seen a ten dollar bill, much less owned one.

"It's a lot of money," Mr. Grover said.

"It's a lot of dog," Skeeter said.

Uncle Jesse looked at the money in the boy's hand and blinked slowly. "That's more than $50. You said $50, and that's more than $50."

"It's $100. It's like Skeeter said—she's a lot of dog and the man I work for is a pretty good fellow and he won't eat me out. The dog is worth every dime of it."

Uncle Jesse looked away then and nobody had anything to say until Mister Cash spoke up. "Suppose you'll be breeding her."

"That's right."

"Then I was just thinking. With all that money maybe Skeeter here could buy one of her puppies."

Mr. Grover was caught off base and didn't know

exactly what to say. One of Lady's puppies would be worth much more than $100, but then, like he had said, the man he worked for was a pretty good fellow and Mr. Grover would see what could be done about it, and told them so.

"No," Skeeter said. "That's rightly nice, but I reckon not. Don't want one of her puppies. Then I'd always be thinking about her. If she's going, then I want her to go and don't always to be thinking about her."

"I know how you feel," Mr. Grover said, and he really did. "I was going to say that I would write you and tell you how she was doing, but I won't do that, son. Because I know how you feel. Maybe, though, you'll be up my way sometime and come around and see us."

"It's a long way," Uncle Jesse said. "A long way up yonder, but now with all that money you might like to go up there and see that country. I'd go with you. I'd like that—going way off up yonder."

The money still was in Skeeter's hand and he continued to stare at it and didn't look up as he spoke. "There just ain't no telling. There just ain't no telling what I might do. Some day I aim to get on a train and go plum' to Atlanta and then just keep going, and going—looking at things."

Uncle Jesse turned his head away and toward the

door of the store and beyond was the swamp, the wild geese flying high and calling and the sandpipers to the wing and away. Mr. Grover felt it, too, and Cash felt it more than he, and they all were silent and then Mr. Grover said, "I suppose it's settled. I'll take the dog on back to Mobile."

"It's settled," Skeeter said. "It's all over."

Mr. Grover stepped to the door and called the dog, calling her Blue, and she turned her head and looked at him and then moved closer to Skeeter and rubbed against his leg. "Come on, Blue." Mr. Grover moved to touch the dog, possibly to pick her up.

Lady snapped at him and Uncle Jesse and Cash exchanged glances and Skeeter rebuked his dog and spoke to Mr. Grover: "She won't follow you."

"Then you lead her out to the truck, will you, son?"

"Ain't I done enough, Mister? Brung my dog in. Want I should be the one to take her out and send her off?"

"No, that's asking too much," Mr. Grover said quickly. "You've done enough."

Again Skeeter looked at the money in his hand and then up at Uncle Jesse and the old man nodded and Skeeter said, "You paid me fair. I'll take her out."

He tossed the money on the counter and spoke to Lady and she followed him willingly out of the door, and Mr. Grover shook hands with Uncle Jesse and Cash Evans and went out, also.

"Hope Lady don't cut up none," Cash said. "The boy's aching and I hope she don't make it no harder on him."

"Things can get just so hard and no harder," Uncle Jesse said. "That Mr. Grover's aching too. Always heard Yankees hard and uppity, but he ain't. He'll do. He's all right if you know him."

"Uh huh, I know. Some are hard and uppity and some ain't. That's how Yankees are. They just can't help it. But I know myself a lot of mighty good Yankees."

"Ain't no use of overdoing it, Cash. Ain't no use of stretching it." Uncle Jesse went to the door and saw that Skeeter was all right, that he and Lady and Mr. Grover were walking toward the truck, and then he went to the back of the store because he didn't want to see the going away.

Mr. Grover said nothing to Skeeter on the way to the truck. He couldn't think of anything to say, but he knew he wanted to be away from there and to try to forget it and knew, too, that he never could. He lowered the tail gate of the truck and there was a crate on the bed of the truck and he nodded toward it. "She goes in there."

"That's what I figured."

"Need any help?"

"No, sir. You go on around and get in the cab and I'll take care of it."

Mr. Grover offered his hand again and they said good-bye to each other and then the man walked around to the cab and Skeeter did not look at Lady at all but opened the door of the crate and spoke to her. "Heah, Lady." She bounded to him. "Up!" She didn't hesitate, but leaped into the crate.

The boy locked the crate and Lady poked her nose through the bars and the boy rubbed her head. She tried to move closer to him, but the bars held her and she tried to nudge them aside and then she clawed at them. A look of fear came into her eyes and she fastened them on the boy, wistfully at first and then pleadingly. There was no bark of protest, no howl of anguish, for her misery was sealed in her throat. Then slowly her eyes filled.

"Don't cry, Lady." The boy reached out to pat her and Mr. Grover, looking back, saw the gesture and thought that it was a signal for him to drive away, and he did and the truck moved off and left the boy standing there in the dust.

Skeeter waited until the truck was out of sight and then he walked back into the store and picked up the money from the counter and went on to the back of the store where Uncle Jesse and Cash were waiting, and Cash said, "They'll take care of her. She's a valuable dog."

"Yes, sir. Reckon so."

"We'll be going on back home whenever you're ready," Uncle Jesse said.

"Never got a chance to shoot over her. Just kept messin' around and showing her off and never got in any real hunting. But I had myself a dog, though."

"Had yourself a dog," Cash said. "Best dog I ever seen and I've seen myself a lot of dogs."

"Best one I ever seen, too." Uncle Jesse nodded his agreement. "You can always say that you had yourself a dog."

The storekeeper reached to a shelf and took down a box of vanilla wafers and passed them around and took one for himself. "Gates was in here early this morning. Me and him thought maybe we'd send ol' Mill over to your place and let you keep him for me. I'll pay good."

"Reckon not," Uncle Jesse said. "We had us a dog."

"But I'll look after him, Uncle Jesse. Be good to have ol' Mill around and I'll do all the work."

"Figured you wouldn't want another dog around."

"I like ol' Mill. He barks and everything, like I'm used to." The boy reached for another of the vanilla wafers. "Lady never did really belong around here. She didn't fit. She'll be better off way up yonder. Yankees feed dogs meat every day. That's what the man told Uncle Jesse."

"Gates will bring ol' Mill over tomorrow if your Uncle Jesse don't mind."

"Don't mind. Whatever the boy wants—well, I don't mind."

Skeeter felt in his pocket where he had put the money and his pocket was bulging and he pulled out the money. "That man said it was $100."

"Heard him," Cash said. Nevertheless, the storekeeper counted it. "That's what it is—$100."

"And how much them Roebuckers cost for Uncle Jesse? Good'uns."

"Good'uns will ruin this $100. Some cheaper, but good'uns come high."

"Now, wait a minute." Uncle Jesse wiped crumbs form his mouth. "We won't do that."

"You heard the boy," Cash said. "He told me to order them Roebuckers and it's his money."

"That's what I said, Uncle Jesse. I told him to order them Roebuckers."

"But I don't want 'em that bad. I just been doing a lot of big-talking about roastin' ears and hicker nuts and things like that. Didn't mean it. I'm doing all right."

"I want the best ones," Skeeter said to Mister Cash. "If it takes ever' cent of that $100, I want the best ones there is."

Uncle Jesse propped his hands on the counter and leaned back and looked over the boy's head and at the beams where the horse collars hung and the plow lines and such as that and knew that he must say no more about it, for a gift must not be debated.

"I'll get good'uns," Mister Cash said. "Order them tonight. And there'll be enough left over, mor'n likely, for a down payment on a .20 gauge."

"That's what I want, if there's enough left over. A little old .20 gauge and me and ol' Mill will hunt us some birds."

Uncle Jesse still was silent and his mind on so many things: the woodbine twining and the sandpiper running into the wind until his wings were steady, and then off and soaring.

Cash Evans raked a match across the sole of his shoe and lit the coal oil stove on which his coffeepot stayed all the time. "Figured a little coffee might go good before y'all went back. Nip in the air."

"I'd like a cup of coffee." Uncle Jesse spoke at last.

Cash got three cups and put them on the counter and soon the coffee was boiling and he filled the cups and reached for a can of condensed milk.

"Drink mine black," Uncle Jesse said.

"I was thinking about Claude."

"Drinks his black, too. Claude does. Black and stout."

The boy watched the men and did exactly as they did and poured some of the coffee into his saucer and blew on it and sipped it. It was very bitter but he drank it all and then he and Uncle Jesse told Mister Cash good-bye and that they'd be seeing him, and they walked out of the store and headed for the swamp and home.

THE END